D1055128

Tia was standing near Ellem's desk. A cloudy mirror hung crookedly on the wall. Clark watched as Tia turned, so her back was toward the mirror.

Clark saw her shrug his flannel shirt from her slender shoulders, then crane her neck so she could see her own reflection.

Clark gasped.

There were no bruises on Tia's back.

But there was something else. Two something elses. Small and translucent green, feathered and webbed with pulsing, darker green veins; they fluttered with every beat of her heart.

Tia Haines had wings.

SMALLVILLE™

#1: *Arrival*

#2: *See No Evil*

#3: *Flight*

#4: *Animal Rage,* arriving February 2003

Available from Little, Brown and Company

Flight

SMALLVILLE™

Flight

Cherie Bennett and Jeff Gottesfeld

Superman created by
Jerry Siegel and Joe Shuster

LITTLE, BROWN AND COMPANY

New York An AOL Time Warner Company

For Alex Taub — a gentleman, a scholar, and the honorary commissioner of the Intergalactic Donkey-Basketball Association (IDBA)

First Edition

ISBN 0-316-17468-8
LCCN 2002110952

10 9 8 7 6 5 4 3 2 1

Q-BF

Printed in the United States of America

CHAPTER 1

Clark Kent frowned as Chloe Sullivan blithely drove around the FULL sign that partially blocked the entrance to the parking lot behind Fordman's department store. "At the risk of stating the obvious," Clark said, "'Full' means: There's no place to park."

"Oh ye of little faith," Pete Ross said from where he sat in the back seat. "Chloe has this covered."

"True," Chloe agreed. She pulled up to the only empty spot in the lot. There was a folding chair in the space. Leaning against the back of the chair was a hand-lettered sign: RESERVED FOR THE PRESS.

Pete scrambled out of the car, moved the chair, and Chloe pulled in.

Clark laughed. "How'd you pull this one off, Chloe?"

"Never underestimate the power of the pen, Clark . . . even that of a school reporter in a tiny place like Smallville. Lex Luthor thinks I have a brilliant journalistic future. I told him I was covering his Smallville Farmer Aid charity carnival for the *Torch*. He volunteered to arrange for my parking space. The rest is history."

She and Clark got out and joined their friend Pete. The three of them headed for Main Street, where the charity carnival was set up.

"At least Luthor's good for something," Pete grumbled.

Clark sighed, knowing only too well how much Pete disliked Lex. It was awkward, because Pete had been Clark's best bud since they were little kids. As for Lex, well, Lex was a newer friend. In some ways, Lex was more like a big brother, since he was a few years older than Clark.

Lex had come to Smallville from Metropolis when his father, Lionel Luthor, had put him in charge of LuthorCorp fertilizer plant in Smallville. The town itself was divided on whether the factory was good or bad for their rural community. It certainly provided a lot of badly needed jobs. But many were convinced it was only a matter of time before Smallville became Luthorville. Lionel's well-earned reputation for cutthroat business practices and an unbridled ego preceded him wherever he went.

Soon after Lex had arrived in Smallville, Clark saved Lex's life. They developed a friendship, and Clark found Lex to be a brilliant, worldly, and loyal friend. And, as Lex so often reminded Clark, just because he was Lionel's son didn't mean that he was anything like Lionel.

I mean, look at this charity carnival, for example, Clark thought as they walked. *A guy who wanted to take over the town wouldn't do this; he'd just buy the farms when they get auctioned by the bank.*

The carnival was in full swing when Clark and his friends stepped onto Main Street. A local band played on a makeshift wooden stage that had been erected in front of the bank. The sidewalks were lined with homemade booths — everything from Soak the Sap to fortune-tellers to balloon darts. Items that had been donated to a silent auction were arrayed on a long table outside the feed store, and teens worked their way through the crowd selling SMALLVILLE CARES raffle tickets.

Pete nudged his elbow into Clark's side. "Check it out."

He cocked his chin toward a kissing booth across the way. Lana Lang was on duty. A line of guys snaked into Main Street, waiting to plunk down their five dollars for a moment with her.

"Figures," Chloe sighed. "If I was in that kissing booth, I'd probably have to pay the guys to kiss me."

Clark shook his head. "You know that's not true."

Chloe put her hands on her hips. "So you're saying you'd wait in line and pay the price of a muffin and cappuccino for the opportunity to kiss me?"

"Of course," Clark agreed gallantly.

Pete cracked up.

"What's so funny?" Clark asked.

"I may have mentioned to Pete that I've got the next shift," Chloe said sweetly. "I'll meet you, your lips, and your wallet over there in an hour. I hope your dad boosted your allowance. For now, I have to hunt for a great journalistic angle on this carnival. See ya." Chloe took off into the crowd.

"She *so* has your number," Pete said, slipping on his sunglasses. "I suppose you want to buy a mess of tickets and get in line for Lana."

"I don't think kissing booths are exactly my speed," Clark decided, as he watched a clerk from the feed store give Lana a peck on the cheek.

Not that I don't want to kiss Lana. I do. But not for charity. And not after a hundred other guys.

And definitely not on the cheek.

Just the thought of Lana filled Clark with feelings he'd never felt toward anyone. And it wasn't the her-parents-were-killed-twelve-years-ago-in-the-meteor-shower thing, either. Well, maybe just a little. Twelve years before, a mysterious meteor shower had rained down on Smallville, wreaking havoc in town. One of those meteorites had exploded on Main Street, killing Lana's mother and father.

All of Smallville — and America — knew about

the day of the meteorites. What people didn't know is that a small spacecraft also crashed to earth in Smallville that day . . . and that the spacecraft carried the toddler "boy" now known as Clark Kent. Jonathan and Martha Kent, who ran a family farm in Smallville, found the spacecraft that day and were ultimately able to adopt the boy as their own.

Of course, no one knew that Clark was anything but human. And no one knew that he had superpowers.

Quite the adoption, Clark thought wryly. *I guess you could say I come from* very *distant relatives. A lot of bad stuff has happened in this town because of those meteors. And I always feel like it's my fault.*

But guilt wasn't what made him care so much about Lana. Nor was it just her transcendent beauty; her dark lustrous hair, or the eyes that seemed to see so much more than what was in front of them. No. His feelings went much deeper, to someplace he was only beginning to know.

The weird thing was, sometimes he got the vibe that she felt exactly the same way about him, even though she had a boyfriend, Whitney Fordman.

As if Lana could read Clark's thoughts, she looked up and waved at him. He waved back, and she beckoned him to join her.

"Come on," Clark told Pete, and they ambled over to Lana's booth.

"How's it going?" Clark greeted Lana, between kisses.

Lana leaned close so that she wouldn't be overheard. "It's insane," she whispered. "In the past forty-five minutes I've been slimed by guys between the ages of ten and death." She checked her watch. "I'm only on for another fifteen minutes. I haven't even seen the carnival yet. Do you two want to check it out with me, or do you already have plans?"

"Where's Whitney?" Pete pointedly asked.

"Working at the store," Lana said. "But last time I checked, we're not joined at the hip."

"Hey, I've been waiting forever for one lousy kiss!" a freckled middle-school kid demanded. "Let's move it!"

"He's not exactly a future heartbreaker," Lana mumbled.

"We'll meet you at the stage in twenty minutes,"

Clark told Lana, and he and Pete headed out. "Good luck."

They decided to make a loop down the street, then circle back. "I can't figure you and Lana out," Pete said as they strolled along.

"Meaning?" Clark asked.

"Meaning you're into her, and she's into you, but she's still with Whitney. It doesn't make sense. Why aren't you two together?"

They passed a little girl and her mother. As they went by, a helium balloon escaped the girl's grasp. It floated skyward, and the little girl cried. Clark didn't hesitate. He jumped straight up — a prodigious vertical leap — and neatly grabbed the string from the bright red balloon in his hand. "Here you go," he told the wide-eyed girl, handing her the balloon after he landed.

"What do you say, Maureen?" her mother sing-songed.

"Thank you."

Pete shook his head as the mom and girl continued on their way. "Man, you got a leap like that, you need to go out for basketball."

Clark shook his head. "I'm a terrible shooter," he fibbed.

The truth, of course, was that he could sink basket after basket from the top of the bleachers if he wanted to. Sometimes it was just so frustrating not to actually *do* it.

"I could work with you on your shot," Pete offered, miming a foul shot. "Anyway, I know that Lana-and-Whitney is the party line. But you two have something going on. Why deny it?"

"I'm not. It's just . . . not that simple." Clark had no idea what else he could possibly say. It *wasn't* simple. He didn't even understand it himself.

"Hey, cool, look at that," Pete said, pointing skyward. Something blue with red, batlike wings swooped and dipped against the azure heavens.

"Is it a bird? Is it a plane? No! It's a Super Kite!" a guy boomed through a megaphone from behind a booth filled with colorful kites. "Super Kites fly higher and faster than any kite ever flew. Get your Super Kites right here, folks!"

"Want a kite, kid?" a voice said from behind Clark. He turned around and saw his mom,

Martha Kent, grinning at him. "You used to love kites when you were little, Clark."

"Uh-oh, serious nostalgia alert," Pete joked.

"Said the boy who once broke his arm while flying a kite," Martha playfully reminded Pete.

Pete grabbed his chest dramatically. "You've wounded my pride, Mrs. Kent."

Martha laughed. "So, this is great, huh?" She looked around at the happy throng. "I think we'll be able to raise some serious money with this crowd. I already sold three dozen homemade pies."

Clark knew his mom had a special interest in the carnival. All over America, family farms were in trouble, and those in Smallville were no exception. Clark could name several farmers whose land had recently been sold at auction. The Kent farm was facing some serious financial challenges, too, but Clark knew his parents would never want help from the carnival proceeds. His dad was far too proud.

Not to mention the fact that my dad doesn't want to have anything to do with taking charity from the Luthors, Clark thought.

"Well, back to my table of baked goods," Martha said, taking off. "Have fun, you two."

As Clark watched his mother walk away, he heard a familiar voice call out. "Clark! Glad you could make it."

Clark turned around to see Lex Luthor approaching him. Clad in black, his bald pate shining in the bright sun, Lex would have stood out in any crowd. Pete scowled in his direction.

"Great turnout, Lex," Clark said, trying to ignore Pete's disapproval.

Lex nodded. "I'm actually quite pleased. I hope we raise a lot of money."

"I bet," Pete snorted sarcastically.

"Pete Ross, your genuine warmth is always a welcome addition to a conversation," Lex said. He never let Pete — or anyone else, for that matter — get to him. "How's your family?"

"You mean my dad? The guy you cheated out of his business?"

"If, in fact, such a thing occurred," Lex began smoothly, "the deed was done by my father, not by me. In fact, Pete, I don't think I've ever harmed you or your family. Or do you want to correct the record?"

Pete didn't answer.

"Raffle tickets!" a boy called, working his way down the street. "Win a computer, or color TV! Tickets are a buck! Thirty for twenty dollars!"

Lex waved him over. "I'll take a book," Lex said, pulling out a twenty.

"Why buy tickets? You donated the prizes, Mr. Luthor," the boy said.

"It's a charitable donation," Lex responded. "Now, go sell some more." The young salesman departed; Lex tore the book in half, giving fifteen tickets to Clark and fifteen to Pete.

"You didn't have to do this," Clark protested.

"Indulge me. It's for a good cause."

"Forget it. I don't want your stupid tickets." Pete tried to hand the torn booklet back to Lex, but Lex waved him off.

"They're not mine now, Pete. They're yours. See you at the drawing, at the bandstand." With an enigmatic smile, Lex turned and waded into the crowd.

"Come on, that was a nice thing for him to do," Clark commented.

"He thinks he can buy people," Pete said darkly.

"You know, Pete, I don't want you take this the wrong way, but I give up," Clark declared. "Lex Luthor could cure cancer and you'd still hate the guy. Come on, let's go meet Lana."

Still fuming, Pete pivoted around, accidentally bumping hard into a teen girl with a blond braid. She stumbled; Clark caught her arm so she wouldn't tumble to the ground.

"Sorry," Pete apologized. "I didn't see you."

"Are you okay?" Clark asked.

She now stood a couple of feet from them, her green eyes darting this way and that in her pale face. Then those eyes met his. Something Clark saw there stopped him cold.

"Are you okay?" Clark repeated.

Barely bobbing her head, the girl seemed to shrink into her oversized sweatshirt, and backed slowly away from them. Then, she turned and dashed away.

Pete looked at Clark. "Okay, was that weird or

was that weird? Where's queen-of-Smallville-weird Chloe when we need her?"

Clark's eyes followed the strange girl through the crowd. "I think I've seen her. At school."

A hundred feet away, the girl turned and looked at Clark over her shoulder. Whoever she was, whatever was going on with her, Clark knew this much:

That girl is scared to death.

Chapter 2

"What did I tell you about going off on your own?" Al Haines growled at his daughter, Tia.

"I'm sorry," Tia mumbled.

"What were you doing over there?"

She'd gone to watch the man demonstrating the Super Kites. Imagining the kites soaring against a powder-blue sky, Tia was filled with longing. But to tell her father this could be very, very dangerous.

"Nothing."

"Haven't I told you time and time again not to wander off on your own?

"I'm sixteen, Dad," she reminded him. "I'm old enough to walk around a carnival by myself."

"It's dangerous," her father insisted. Her older brother, Kyle, nodded in emphatic agreement.

"You stay close to the family," Kyle said.

Sometimes, Tia wanted to scream . . . and never stop screaming. She'd been so looking forward to the carnival, even if she did have to be there with her father and brother. At least it was someplace new. Her entire life revolved around school, her part-time job, and cleaning their house.

She couldn't believe her situation. She wasn't ugly — sometimes she thought she could even be seen as cute. Yet she was a high school junior with no friends and no life. All because of the family secret.

She'd lived with the secret since she was a little girl. It had been drummed into her head: If anyone finds out, they'll take you away from the family.

She couldn't help herself. She sneaked a look at the two guys who just helped her. The tall one, with the dark hair, was so handsome. The shorter one had the nicest, sweetest smile. She'd seen them at school but had no idea what their names were. For just a moment, Tia imagined that they were her friends. She could keep the secret from them, she was sure she could.

"You know, Tia, all I'm doing is protecting the family," her father said, his voice kinder now. "You want them to study you like animals in the zoo?"

"No."

"You want them to take you away from me and your brother, just when we're making money in the stock market? We moved to a real nice home, didn't we?"

She nodded. Her father had painted vivid, nightmarish pictures of this scenario for as long as she could remember. The idea filled her with terror. It was true — they did seem to have a lot more money lately. But it was also true that if the secret ever got out, their family would be ruined.

Her father tugged playfully on the end of her braid. "Time to go."

Dutifully, she followed them to the car. What choice did she have? But it was all just so unfair.

ꕥ ꕥ ꕥ ꕥ

"I'm glad that's finished," Lana said, joining Clark and Pete. She rubbed at her cheek. "That kid with the freckles practically suctioned my skin off. Ick."

"Still looks good to me," Clark said lightly. "Which way do you want to go?"

Lana pulled out a fistful of raffle tickets. "Lex did the sweetest thing before. He gave me these."

"Us, too," Clark said.

"Well, the raffle is in, like, five minutes," Lana told them. "Let's see if we win anything."

By the time they arrived, a crowd had already gathered around the stage. Janet Barkley, the current reigning Miss Smallville, stood with Lex. Everyone knew Janet. She'd been homecoming queen for two straight years before she went off to Metropolis University. She was already certified as a commercial aviator and planned to become an airline pilot. In the Miss Kansas pageant, held just a month or so before in Topeka, Janet had placed fifth.

Janet leaned toward the microphone, her Miss Smallville sash rustling. "Get ready for the first drawing," she declared. "Call out if you've got the winning number on your tickets!"

She waited a short moment as people found their raffle tickets, then she and Lex reached together into the giant glass bowl that contained the winning numbers. In turn, they announced winners of gift certificates, computers and TVs, dinner for two at a fancy Metropolis restaurant, and a month of free coffee at the Talon.

"Now, we have an unusual prize," Janet continued. "The next two winners will get a free skydiving session, including a first jump from an airplane. I'll be piloting the plane; my partner will be your jump instructor. He promises to be gentle," she added, to chuckles from the crowd, then reached into the bowl and pulled out a ticket. "Ticket 372!"

"Me!" Pete yelped, waving his ticket in the air. "I won! I'm 372!" Pete worked his way up to the stage, where Janet handed him his winner's certificate.

"This is so cool, I never won anything before," Pete said, beaming.

Janet reached into the bowl again, then called, "Ticket 281!"

Lana sagged. "My tickets go from 270 to 280. Too bad. I'd love to jump out of an airplane, wouldn't you?"

"Oh yeah. Definitely," Clark agreed.

Of course, that's a big, fat lie, Clark thought. *I'd sooner dance on those green meteorites that make me feel so sick than jump out of an airplane.*

He'd been afraid of heights for as long as he could remember. He knew it was ridiculous, considering that he could do stuff like step in front of a rampaging city bus or dodge a bullet. He knew it was irrational. Nuts, in fact. But that didn't change how he felt.

"One more time, number 281!" Janet called again. "If no one claims it, I'll choose another number."

Clark happened to glance down. There, a few feet ahead of him, was a fallen raffle ticket. It was facedown. He blasted with his X-ray vision, so he could see through it and view the ink on the bottom side.

Ticket 281. Someone must have dropped it. Maybe even Lana, when she'd taken her tickets out. He looked around to see if anyone seemed to be missing a ticket, but no one did. So, pretending to retie his sneaker, he surreptitiously pushed it under Lana's left shoe, flipping it as he did.

"Lana, I think you're standing on one," Clark said innocently, as he stood up.

She looked down and saw ticket 281. "It's me!" Lana cried in surprise. "I must have dropped it. Hey! I have 281!"

"We have a winner," Lex told the crowd. "Miss Lana Lang!"

Lex helped her up onto the platform, where Janet handed her the skydiving gift certificate. Clark had to smile watching Lana; she looked so excited.

After the other big prizes had been given out, Pete and Lana rejoined Clark. Pete pulled a packet of instructions about the skydiving experience from his prize envelope.

"It says here the jump will happen at the Smallville airstrip," he read. "Let's see. There's a day of instruction and then the jump. 'This prize package is worth three hundred dollars.' Too cool! You and me, Lana."

Lana looked thoughtful. "I was thinking. I know

how much Clark wants to do this. Maybe we can go together."

"Oh, that's okay," Clark said quickly.

"But I distinctly heard you tell me how much you want to skydive, " Lana reminded him. "And if it weren't for you, I wouldn't even have known I was standing on the winning ticket."

"Lana's right," Pete agreed. "We wouldn't want to leave you out of the fun, Clark. Up there, really, really high, jumping from an airplane . . ."

Clark felt like killing Pete. After all, Pete *knew* Clark was afraid of heights.

"So, Pete, how about the three of us splitting the cost of Clark's joining in?" Lana suggested. "It's three hundred dollars, so that would mean it'll only cost a hundred each. I'd say that's a bargain."

"I couldn't let you do that," Clark began.

"It's already done. Right, Pete?" Lana asked.

"Right!" Pete clapped Clark on the back to seal the deal.

"But . . . um . . . I don't have the money," Clark stammered.

"We'll work it out," Lana said.

"Yeah," Pete agreed. "I bet Janet will let us do a payment plan."

"Uh, but . . ." Clark stammered. "Maybe your parents won't let you, Pete."

"Are you kidding? Two of my uncles were paratroopers."

Clark was going down fast. He turned to Lana. "And what about Nell? It's kind of risky, don't you think?" Lana had been raised by her Aunt Nell, who was very protective of Lana since her parents died in the meteor shower twelve years ago.

"If anyone but Janet was in charge, she'd probably give me a hard time," Lana allowed. "But Nell wants me to *be* Janet. She'll definitely say yes."

"Oh," Clark managed. "Well, good."

"Great! Then it's settled." Lana's dark eyes danced with excitement. "Just think, Clark: all of us up there with the birds. It's as close as we'll ever come to flying."

Chapter 3

Out in the barn behind the Kent farmhouse, Clark held the tractor wagon aloft and on its side as if it were a toy, while his father, Jonathan, worked on one of the axles. There was hay in the fields ready to be cut and brought in. Without the wagon, it would be impossible. Jonathan muttered as he worked, which meant it wasn't going well . . . which Clark knew also meant it was less than the perfect time to ask him about getting a part-time job.

But, since time was of the essence, Clark couldn't put it off. As for Martha, she'd already said yes — but contingent on Jonathan's agreement.

"Okay, let 'er down," Jonathan instructed as he stepped carefully out of the way. "Can you get me the lug wrench, son? And what's this about a sudden interest in joining the work force?"

Clark gulped. Clearly his mother had spoken to his dad, who was now beating Clark to the punch.

"I'd just like to make some money on my own, Dad. I'm not a kid anymore. And it's not sudden. I've given it a lot of thought." He got the lug wrench and gave it to his dad.

Well, that is sort of true. Every time I get my allowance, I feel bad taking money they desperately need for the farm.

His dad silently tightened the lugs on the wagon, then found a rag with which to wipe his hands. "Well, if you were going to work, what kind of job would you be thinking about?"

Clark shrugged. "Whatever I can get, I guess. I saw a Help Wanted sign in the window of Smallville Pizza."

Jonathan looked pensive. "I don't know if this is such a good idea. You'd have to hide your powers, obviously. You might think that's going to be easy, but you're going to be tempted to use them to make the work easier. Anyone would."

"Well, it's not like I have a choice about that,"

Clark pointed out. "I'm going to have to deal with it my whole life — as far as we know, anyway. I'm growing up, Dad. I've got to spread my wings and fly just like any other kid."

"Except that you're not like any other kid," his dad said softly.

"Yes, he is," came Martha's firm voice, as she joined them.

"I take it you heard me," Jonathan said.

Martha nodded. "And it's not as if you didn't make sense. But Clark's right, too. When it comes to work, he'll have to do it like any other kid, without any powers." She looked at her son. "You're not going to enjoy that, you know."

"You guys underestimate me," Clark insisted. "I think I'll love it. Besides, I'm highly motivated."

"Ah. The other shoe drops. You need money for something specific," his dad guessed, then he grinned. "No, no, and *no*. You are not going to reggae SunSplash in Jamaica. Not until you're in college. Make that graduate school. Make that when you're on Medicare."

"He won't need Medicare," Martha reminded her husband.

"True. But you get my point," Jonathan said.

Clark grinned. "It's not for Jamaica." Then, he told his folks about how Lana and Pete wanted to include him on their skydiving adventure.

"Am I hearing this correctly?" Martha wondered. "The boy who's afraid of heights wants to jump out of an airplane?"

"It's the perfect way for me to conquer my fear, don't you think?" Clark bluffed.

"Jonathan? What do you think about skydiving?" Martha asked.

"Well, if there's anyone in the universe it's safe for, it's Clark," Jonathan mused.

"So I can do it?" Clark queried. "And get a job, too?"

Jonathan scratched his day-old beard. "No more than three evenings a week. If your grades fall or you don't do your chores, or we find out we need you here at the farm, the deal is off."

"Sold," Clark agreed, and put out his hand for his dad to shake.

The deal sealed, Clark super-sped back to the house and to his bathroom. There was no time to waste. He'd shower, change, then head downtown to find a job.

This is going to be so great. The job part, anyway.

ꕥꕥꕥꕥ

"You pick up your apron here, and clock in over there," Max McSorley told Clark as he led him through the back kitchen area of Smallville Pizza. Clark dutifully tied on the busboy apron that Max handed him and followed his new boss to the time clock. Max gave him a card, told him to write his name on it, and then showed him how to punch in and out.

Clark knew a little about Max, who was one of Smallville's more colorful characters. He had once been the best welterweight fighter in his native Scotland; after a brief boxing career, he came to Smallville to live with some cousins and his father.

First, he tried opening a Scottish restaurant, but no one seemed to have a taste for sheep's intestine and warm beer. Then, when Smallville Pizza went up for sale, Max and his cousins bought it. They learned the pizza business and turned the place into a modest success, although Clark knew that the Talon was starting to attract its customers.

When Clark had applied for a job, he hadn't expected to start five minutes later. But Saturday night was Max's busiest night and one of his waiters had just quit.

"Don't suppose you know anything about making pizza?" Max asked hopefully, with his soft Scottish brogue, as he led Clark past the giant baking ovens.

"No, sir, Mr. McSorley."

"Call me Ellem, like the rest of the world does," he invited. "L for Little, M for Max. Me father back there is Big Max." He cocked his head toward a beefy man scattering pepperoni over an unbaked pizza. "I know you don't have experience bussing or waiting tables, because you told me this is your first job," Ellem continued, not looking any too happy about it. "Well, never mind. I didn't know me bum from a fried egg when I started, either."

"I'm a quick study," Clark assured him.

"Good. You'll be proving it." Ellem slapped an order pad in Clark's palm. "So, you take the order, write it down and put it up here." Max flipped a beefy hand toward the counter that divided the kitchen from the restaurant. "Don't slip your order in front of anyone else's, no matter what."

Clark nodded. It sounded easy, really.

Ellem took him to the cash register, where a menu was posted. "Ever worked a register? Of course not," Ellem went on, answering his own question. "For the love of Pete, why don't they ever teach you kids anything useful in school?"

"Pick up!" Big Max boomed, sliding a pizza onto the counter, next to two others that were already there. "Jesus, Joseph, and Mary, you're two pies behind, Marie!"

"You think I can't see that?" An attractive woman in her thirties, with caramel skin and a halo of dark curls, bustled over. "I have two hands and ten fingers and I can only do what I can do." She hoisted the pie onto a tray, and then onto her raised palm. "Don't blame me if people walk out, Ellem," she warned over her shoulder.

"No worries, Marie, this young man has come to save the day," Ellem called to her. He tapped Clark on the back. "Well, no time like the present. Get out there and take some orders!"

Clark stepped onto the floor of the restaurant. Almost every table was full, but only half of them had any food. He picked the table of people who looked hungriest and went to it.

"Hi, I'm Clark, I'll be your —"

"*Finally!*" the dad interrupted. "It's been fifteen minutes. What do you kids want?" There were four young boys at the table with him, and they started shouting out demands. Meanwhile, Clark felt a tug at his arm and turned around.

"Hey, waiter?" a middle-aged man seated with his wife and two children asked Clark. "Where's our food? If I wanted to wait to eat, I'd go to Metropolis."

"I'll go check. " Clark turned to the dad. "Be right back." The man looked like a drowning victim whose raft had just been snatched away.

Clark headed for the kitchen, but neither Big

Max nor Ellem were anywhere in sight. The only person Clark could see was a chef with a long blond braid. Her back was to him as she slid a pizza from the oven.

"Um, excuse me!" Clark called out to her. "Are these two pepperoni pizzas up for table, er . . . eight?"

"Check the order slips," the girl said as she turned around. Her cheeks were flushed from the heat of work, but Clark recognized her right away.

It was the girl from the carnival. She didn't look happy.

"Hi. We met at the carnival," Clark reminded her. "I'm —"

"We're not supposed to socialize at work." She went back to the oven.

I wouldn't exactly call a name exchange "socializing," Clark thought.

The next few hours passed in a blur. Ellem and Big Max spent most of the night hollering, and Marie hollered back. The girl with the braid hardly ever opened her mouth. A few people walked out in a huff because they had to wait too long for their pizzas.

For Clark, it was frustrating. He knew that if someone would just show him the technique, he could make a hundred pizzas in an hour and wait on all the customers, too. But instead, he had to plod along in what felt like super-slow motion.

The place closed at midnight. Marie showed Clark the drill for closing up: sweep and mop, wash down all the stainless steel kitchen surfaces, refill the parmesan cheese, salt, garlic, and pepper shakers on every table. The list went on, and Clark dutifully went through it, again knowing that he could have the place spotless in seconds if only he could use his powers. Meanwhile, the girl with the braid chopped vegetables and refilled the vats inside the industrial-sized refrigerator. Ellem and Big Max were in the restaurant's tiny office, doing who-knows-what.

Clark twisted open another grated cheese shaker and filled it. "What's the girl's name who works in the kitchen?" he asked Marie.

"Tia," Marie said as she wiped down a table. "She's a funny one."

"Why do you say that?"

"You'll see. Her father or her big brother will

be here any minute. They give me the creeps. Hey, get me some more paper towels, will you?"

"Sure." Clark went through the kitchen and into the back room where paper goods and cleaning supplies were stored. To his great surprise, Tia was there.

Reading a book.

She jumped up, hid the book behind her back, and pressed herself into the corner.

"Sorry," Clark said. "I didn't mean to startle you. I need to get —"

He stopped. She looked so scared. He started again, his voice friendly and gentle. "I guess I should introduce myself. I'm Clark Kent. Marie told me your first name is Tia. But she didn't tell me your last name."

"Haines." Red circles of embarrassment blotched her pale cheeks.

"Nice to meet you, Tia Haines. I hear you make a heck of a pizza. And I think I've seen you at Smallville High. Right?"

Tia nodded warily.

Clark plunged on. "So . . . how long have you been working here?"

"A few months." She cleared her throat. "I should go." She eyed the door, which Clark was blocking.

"I just came in for paper towels," Clark explained. He stepped aside so Tia could exit. As she got ready to depart, she slipped the book under the waistline in the back of her apron.

Okay. That is not normal, Clark thought. *What could she possibly be reading that she has to keep secret?*

"Tia!" a deep, male voice bellowed.

Clark watched as a middle-aged man with red-rimmed eyes burst into the kitchen. He eyed the storage room, looking from Tia to Clark and back again. "What are you two doing?"

"Nothing, Dad," Tia said.

Mr. Haines glared at Clark. "You're the kid from the carnival. What do you want with my daughter?"

"We both work here. That's all." Clark had a hard time keeping the anger out of his voice. But Mr. Haines's attitude was getting on his nerves.

"Clark just started tonight," Tia added.

"Martha and Jonathan's boy?" Mr. Haines asked.

Clark nodded. He could see Tia's back, and he

knew her father couldn't. He gulped. The book she'd hidden in her waistband began to slide down. Any second it would fall. Clark sensed Tia freezing in panic. For whatever reason, she was absolutely petrified of having her dad catch her with that book.

"Sir, watch out, behind you!" Clark yelled.

Mr. Haines whirled around. In a flash of super-speed, Clark caught the book as it fell and slipped it under a nearby pile of soiled tablecloths.

By the time Mr. Haines turned back, Clark had assumed the same stance he'd had a moment before.

"What?" Mr. Haines asked him. "There's nothing there."

"Sorry, sir," Clark said. "I thought I saw. . ." Clark's mind was a total blank.

"Marie coming, with the mop bucket," Tia invented quickly.

Mr. Haines frowned. "Clock out and get your stuff, Tia. Kyle's waiting."

Tia dutifully did as her father told her, and Clark took the paper towels out to Marie. As Tia left the restaurant, she shot Clark a look of immense gratitude.

Clark didn't hesitate. The moment she was gone, he went back to the kitchen and unearthed the book she'd been so desperate to keep secret. On the cover was a bird, wings spread, soaring over a perfect beach. The title was odd. Clark had never heard of it.

Jonathan Livingston Seagull.

CHAPTER 4

Whitney Fordman leaned over the department store receipts and rubbed his eyes. When he had been a kid, picturing his future, he had never imagined this. He was the jock king of Smallville High. Football scouts from really good colleges were expressing an interest in him; he'd been on top of the world, invincible.

And then, everything changed. His dad got sick. Really sick. His mom had to run the family department store on her own. And it didn't look as if Whitney could apply to college. Now, here he was, stuck in the back office on a Saturday night, tallying up the week's receipts. Men's underwear was having a banner week, but kids' shoes were down.

He would have laughed if it didn't feel so pathetic.

But he thought: *Hey, when it comes to family, you do what you have to do.*

Lana told him over and over how much she respected him for working so hard at Fordman's. But how would she feel if he ended up like the losers who hung out at the auto body shop, reliving their glory days of scoring touchdowns for the Smallville Crows because that was as good as their lives were ever going to get? No, he couldn't tell her any of that.

He glanced at the clock. It was after midnight. Arrayed before him were piles of cash, checks, and credit card slips. Every Saturday night he'd total up these receipts, fill out a deposit slip, and take the deposit to the night drop of Smallville Savings and Loan.

There was just one more calculation he had to do: the overall total monies taken in for the week. Whitney input the numbers into his adding machine. Then he did it again, hoping the figures would match. They did. He notated the totals, signed the deposit slip, and snapped rubber bands around the cash, checks, and other deposit materials. Then, he put it all into the heavy-duty canvas deposit bag.

The bank was just on the other side of the street, so there was no sense taking his pickup truck. After locking up and setting the alarm system, he slung the deposit bag over his shoulder and started to cross Main Street. He kind of liked being downtown this late. No one was around. It was almost as if Smallville were some deserted movie set of a small town.

A gust of wind blew up from behind, mussing his hair. He didn't think anything of it. Hey, this was Kansas. The wind swirled all the time.

But a moment later, Whitney got smashed facedown to the ground by another burst of wind — truly out of the ordinary. So was the unseen assailant who pinned him to the concrete. Whitney flailed, trying to fight off his attacker. But he was helpless. When he opened his mouth to scream, he felt a rag stuffed into his mouth. Still facedown on the pavement, he could not see his attacker. Then with a whoosh of wind, whatever had tackled him to the ground was gone.

Panting from fear, shaking with adrenaline, Whitney sat up. He pulled the rag from his mouth — it was a T-shirt. He looked around. Nothing. No sign of his attacker. Or attackers. Something on the concrete fluttered, and he bent down to see what it was. A few dark green feathers were strewn about. Whatever. No clue at all. But for some reason he stuck a few feathers in his pocket.

Then a sick feeling came over him as he realized that the deposit bag was gone. Thousands of dollars in receipts. Gone.

Finally, he got up from the concrete, went to his truck, and drove the few blocks to the police station. But even as he pulled into the parking lot, he wondered what he would tell them:

"Yes, I was mugged and robbed. But they didn't leave a mark on me, and I didn't see a thing."

Who would believe him? Heck, he barely believed it himself.

CHAPTER 5

"Clark, are you sure you don't want us to wait for you?" Pete asked as he chomped on another slice of pizza. He, Chloe, and Lana had come to Smallville Pizza for a late-night snack.

Clark shook his head. "Thanks anyway. I'm closing tonight, which means I'll be really late. First time. I want to make sure I get it all right."

"One week on the job, already you're the fair-haired boy," Chloe said, wiping tomato sauce from her mouth. "You lead a charmed life, Clark."

"If I led a charmed life I'd win the lottery instead of spending my evenings mopping up pizza gunk."

"Good point," Chloe agreed. "But it's for a worthy cause — the thrill of falling through the atmosphere, the only things separating you and death being a few strings and some puffy material. *Quelle* poetic."

Clark felt his stomach somersault.

"It's actually very safe," Lana said.

"Can you sit with us for a while, Clark?" Chloe asked, scooting over in the booth.

"Just for a minute," Clark said, sliding in next to Chloe. Business was slow at that moment — as it turned out, other than Saturday nights, it was almost always slow. Not only that, Ellem was proving to be an easy guy to work for.

Clark turned to Lana. "How's Whitney doing?" he asked. He'd heard about the robbery, of course. Everyone had heard of the robbery. He'd also heard that the police were intensely skeptical of Whitney's story, so much so that they were considering Whitney himself as a suspect.

Lana put down her half-eaten pizza slice. "Not well. It's been more than a week. You'd think the police would have come up with *something.*"

"It's really messed up for them to just accuse him like that," Pete said.

Lana took a sip of her diet cola. "I thought you

were innocent until proven guilty. It seems like the police have decided he's guilty until proven innocent. I can't believe they'd think he'd steal his own family's money."

"It's just bizarre that Whitney didn't see who attacked him." Chloe mused. Then she perked up. "Hey, maybe it's that invisible —"

Everyone groaned. "No more invisibility!" Pete exclaimed. "I've had it with invisibility."

Chloe folded her arms. "Might I remind you that in Smallville, bizarre woo-woo things happen on a somewhat regular basis," she declared. "We don't get to pick the woo-woo of our choice."

Pete blew the cover of his straw at her.

"Well, do you have a better theory?" Chloe challenged. "The best thing for Whitney is that there have been two similar robberies, one in Smallville and one in Middletown, which is all of ten miles away. Both at night, neither victim saw the attacker. I'm open to all theories from the peanut gallery."

"You're right about the other attacks taking the suspicion off of Whitney," Clark agreed.

Lana made a face. "Except that the only evidence the cops have — the T-shirt they stuffed in his mouth — is from Fordman's store."

"Ouch," Clark grimaced.

"Tell me about it," Lana agreed.

"Order up!" Tia called, setting a fresh pie on the counter.

Pete nabbed the last slice on the table and eyed Tia. "She still from Planet Strange?"

"Maybe she's just shy," Lana suggested.

"Oh, I forgot to tell you, Clark," Chloe said, rooting around in her backpack. She pulled out a copy of *Jonathan Livingston Seagull.* "Ta-da! That book you asked about? Got it from the library."

Clark sneaked a look at Tia, whose back was turned. He'd told his friends about the book Tia had hidden from her dad. Now, though, with Chloe waving *Jonathan Livingston Seagull* around, he felt as if he had somehow betrayed a confidence.

"Did you read it?"

Chloe nodded. "Cover to cover, which took all of, like, an hour. It's one of those psychobabble books. This one gull is different from the other gulls, and he has trouble flying. So when he, like, learns to embrace his differences and believe in himself, he can fly." Chloe rolled her eyes. "How *Oprah* is that?"

Pete plucked it from Chloe's hands. "Hey, I know this book. My dad told me that when he was in high school, everyone read it. I think he got his first date with my mom by quoting it. Wait. Maybe that was *Love Story.*"

Chloe took back the book. "The point is, why would Tia need to hide this from dear old dad?"

"I have no idea," Clark admitted. "But when I gave it back to her the next day, it was like I'd found her lost diary or something."

"Clark, you chatting or working?" Marie asked, as she blew by with a super-size veggie special.

Clark rose. "Gotta get back to work, guys. Thanks for stopping in. And please, no matter what you do, don't leave a tip."

♋♋♋♋

You're sure you two can handle this?" Ellem asked Clark and Tia. "Because if you feel nervous in any way, I'll cancel me card game and —"

"It's fine, Ellem," Tia assured him. "That midnight poker game has your name all over it."

"Right," Clark agreed. It amazed him how easily Tia seemed to talk to Ellem and Big Max, when she was so ill at ease with people her own age.

Since he'd returned her book to her, she'd gotten a little bit friendlier. She told Clark that her family had recently moved from a modest place outside of town to a new home in the LuthorCorp housing development, where she had her own room for the first time.

When Clark asked why she'd been so nervous about having her father see the book, she'd stammered out something about his being the kind of parent who thought he had the right to monitor everything his kids read or saw on TV.

But I know that's not it, Clark thought. *She's lying. I just don't know why.*

Clark had also noticed that Tia never mentioned her mom.

"All right, then," Ellem decided. "You're good kids, I trust you. I'll take the receipts, so you won't have to worry about the midnight thief striking," he added with a wink. "Night, all."

After Ellem departed, Clark did the backup work on the restaurant floor. Again, the tediousness was overwhelming. Unscrew each saltshaker. Pour salt from the big box. Replace the cap. Over and over and over. Same with the black pepper. Same with garlic powder. Fill the napkin containers. . . .

Clark looked down at the napkin holder he'd just replenished. Clark realized he'd filled it backward. He checked out the other tables. Oh no. He'd been so bored he'd filled them *all* backward.

He glanced toward the kitchen. Tia wasn't there. Perfect. He knew if he moved quickly enough —

Bam! Clark super-sped from one table to the next; in a split second, all the napkin containers had been refilled and replaced properly. Then, unable to resist the urge, he zoomed around the room, lifting off glass tops, pulling out soiled tablecloths, replacing them with snowy white fresh ones, resetting the glass tops, wiping them down with cleaner and paper towels. Wow. It felt so good just to move!

He was about to do a super-sweep and super-mop of the floor, when he stopped. Something smelled funny.

Smoke.

In a blur, he was in the kitchen, where flames from the big eight-burner gas stove leaped skyward. Tia was struggling with the fire extinguisher, aiming at the flames.

"Tia!"

"I can do it!"

He grabbed for the extinguisher, but she wrenched it away. The motion jerked her off balance; she stumbled backward into the shooting flames. Her baggy T-shirt and chef's apron ignited instantly.

As she screamed in terror, Clark turned the extinguisher on her, putting out the flames. Then, shielded by smoke from the fire, he crimped the gas line leading to the stove so that no more gas could burn.

He went to Tia. She lay on her back, looking dazed. "Are you okay?" he asked.

"Don't look!" Suddenly, she scuttled backward into the corner like some kind of bizarre four-legged bug.

Maybe the back of her T-shirt burned away and she's embarrassed, Clark figured.

He took off his own flannel shirt and held it out to her. "It's okay. Here. Put this on."

She didn't move. He came closer, still holding out his shirt.

"You're sure you don't have any burns?" Clark asked.

"I'm sure."

He spoke slowly and moved a bit closer. "I know you had a big scare, but —"

"Get away," she croaked hoarsely. "Get away from me."

It was clear to Clark that she was terrified. And suddenly, he knew.

Her father beats her. She's got marks on her back and she doesn't want me to see them.

His stomach recoiled at the thought. But having met Mr. Haines, he was sure his theory was on the money. He spoke very gently to her, inching toward her.

"Tia. It's okay. I won't hurt you. I know what's going on."

She sagged down the wall, now, curled into a ball, knees pulled up to her chest. "Please," she whimpered. "Please. Don't."

"Shh. It's okay. I won't hurt you. I promise. I *promise.*"

He was close enough to touch her now. But he didn't. He just held out his shirt.

She reached up for it and pulled it on, then rose to her feet. "Thank you," she managed.

"You're welcome. How did the fire start?"

"I don't know. Some problem with the gas. That stove was turned to 'off.'"

"Maybe we should get you over to the hospital, just to be sure —"

She checked the bottom of her braid for singe, and it wasn't too bad. "Really. I'm okay."

Clark was certain that wasn't true. Yet he couldn't very well accuse her father of child abuse without any proof, could he?

"You put the fire out before there was really any damage," Tia went on, sounding stronger now. "I'm sure Ellem is insured. I hope."

“It was my fault,” Clark said quickly. “I should have been back here.”

“No. That’s nice of you to say, but I can’t let you take the fall.”

“Well, we can share it, how’s that?” Clark suggested. “I don’t know where Ellem’s card game is, so we should probably call Big Max at home. I mean, I don’t think we should just leave.”

She nodded. “I’ve got his number. I’ll call him. Do you think he’ll fire me?”

“Don’t worry. I’ll vouch for you.”

She rewarded him with a luminous smile. “Thank you. For so many things.” She hesitated. “You’ve been really nice to me. I don’t know why, but —”

“I think you deserve to be treated better than what you’re used to,” Clark said, hoping he was giving her the opening to talk about her father.

But she didn’t. She just nodded.

He gave it one last try. “So, if you ever want to talk . . .”

“Everything’s fine,” she insisted, and, as she did, Clark could almost *see* her personal-boundaries wall go back up. “I’ll go call Big Max.” She went into Max and Ellem's personal office, and closed the door.

Clark wrestled with his conscience. Tia was obviously a very private person. But he felt so sure about what her father was doing that he knew he had to find the evidence. It was the only way he could really help her.

He concentrated hard, aiming his energy toward the door to his bosses' office, and through it, until he saw Tia with his X-ray vision. She was standing near Ellem's desk. A cloudy mirror hung crookedly on the wall. Clark watched as Tia turned, so her back was toward the mirror.

Clark saw her shrug his flannel shirt from her slender shoulders, then crane her neck so she could see her own reflection.

Clark gasped.

There were no bruises on Tia's back.

But there was something else. Two something elses. Small and translucent green, feathered and webbed with pulsing, darker green veins; they fluttered with every beat of her heart.

Tia Haines had wings.

CHAPTER 6

Clark was the first to arrive at the Talon. As they'd planned, he took a table in the back and waited for Tia. For once, Clark was glad to find that Lana was not around. He needed to concentrate on what he wanted to say.

The night before, he and Tia had waited together for Big Max to arrive. At first, Max was angry. But when he saw there hadn't actually been much damage and that the culprit for the fire was a broken valve, he calmed down.

And all the time I was talking to Big Max, I was trying to figure out what to do about Tia, Clark recalled. *But what could I possibly have said? "Say, Tia, I have X-ray vision and I was actually using it to spy on you, and I couldn't help noticing that you've got green wings growing out of your back. What's up with that?"*

So, instead, Clark had simply asked her to meet him at the Talon at noon the next day. Now, as he waited for her, he drummed his fingers nervously on the table, unsure of what to say when she got there.

At least I understand now why she's reading Jonathan Livingston Seagull.

"Hi, Clark." Tia slid into the booth across from him. "I hope I'm not late. I had to take the bus."

"I just got here," he assured her.

"Oh. Okay." She smiled shyly. "I'm glad you invited me."

Her eyes were shining. She was wearing pale pink lipstick—he'd never seen her with any makeup on before.

That's when it hit him. She thought this was a date.

Okay. I'm the biggest idiot in the entire state of Kansas. I have absolutely no idea how to handle this. Not that she isn't pretty, because she is. And nice. And who am I to quibble about some minor physical . . . differences.

"Wow, it's crowded. Nice, though," Tia said, looking around. "I've never been here. Doesn't your friend Lana run it or something?"

Clark nodded.

"Well, I like it. I'd like it even if it were a cave, to tell you the truth. I never get to go anywhere, actually. My father . . . well, he's kind of strict." She unconsciously wet her lips. "I'm babbling, huh?"

"No, you're fine," Clark assured her.

"I guess I'm kind of nervous."

"Do you want some coffee?" Clark asked, stalling for time as he tried to figure out what he wanted to say.

Tia wrinkled her nose. "Hate it."

"How about a walk?" Clark suggested. "It's so nice outside."

They got up and left the place. When they were outside, Tia exulted. "Mmm, the air smells so fresh, huh?" She threw her arms open wide and twirled around in a circle. "I feel great!"

I have to tell her. I have to come right out and —

Tia almost skipped down Main Street. "You know, Clark," she confided, "I didn't tell my dad about this." They waited for a red light to change.

"Why not?"

She shrugged. "He worries about me."

"He seems kind of . . . stern," Clark said, choosing his words carefully.

"Tell me about it," she agreed as they crossed the street. "He was still asleep and I left him a note. I've never done that before."

"I'd say you're in safe company. It's a Sunday and you're in downtown Smallville. I don't think he could get too upset about that."

"Right." She nodded emphatically.

In silence, the two of them continued down Main Street, finally reaching the high school. When the sidewalk ended, Clark knew he couldn't wait any longer.

"I have to tell you something, Tia."

"Okay."

"I . . ." Clark exhaled deeply. "I know about your wings."

Tia stopped. All the color drained from her face.

"It's okay," he quickly added. "I just had to tell you that I know."

"You're going to tell, aren't you?" Tia whispered. "I'm a freak."

"No. Tia —"

"Yes, I am," she insisted. "You must be disgusted."

"*No,*" Clark said firmly. "Does your father know?"

Tia shook her head.

"That's what you're trying to keep hidden from him, isn't it?"

She grabbed his arm, panicking. "You can't tell him."

"I won't."

"You can't tell *anyone*. Ever!"

He looked deeply into her eyes. One part of him longed to tell her that he had his own secrets, secrets that were potentially just as damaging to his life — maybe even more so — than her secrets were to her. The other part of him knew that to say such a thing would be absolute folly.

Finally, he compromised with himself.

"Tia. Listen to me. I understand that there are some things the world doesn't need to know. Trust me. I will never tell."

Something about his tone of voice seemed to reassure her. There was a park bench nearby. She sat, her body sagging. "It's so hard to keep a really big secret." She fisted away a tear as it rolled down her cheek. "It takes so much effort."

I understand that better than you will ever know.

Clark sat next to her.

"It makes me feel so alone. Do you ever feel that way?" she asked.

"Yeah," Clark said, nodding. "I have this loft in our barn — it's kind of my private space. I keep my telescope up there. Sometimes when I really feel alone, I go there and think about how vast the universe is . . . and somehow it makes me feel less alone. Looking at the stars like that."

Tia nodded. She was silent for a long moment. "The wings started growing a few months ago," she confessed, staring at the ground.

"Were you scared?"

"Yes. But I was happy, too."

Clark was surprised at that. His face must have showed it.

Tia raised her face and offered him a shy smile. "My mother had wings, too, you see."

"Your mother —?" Clark faltered.

"Right after the meteor shower, my mother grew wings. I remember it, even though I was only three. My mom was outside, hanging out laundry, when a meteorite exploded against our garage. Right after that we all got this weird green rash on our backs. My mom was closest to the meteorite when it hit. She was covered in dust.

"A few months later, her wings began to grow, like some kind of . . . I don't know . . . mutation. It started as a strange little ridge of feathers at the small of her back. I got a ridge on my back then, too. But only recently, mine started to grow like hers had."

Clark felt as if someone had punched him in the stomach. If the meteorites had caused this, then *he* had caused this.

"Tia, where were you that day?"

"My father says I was outside playing. I don't really remember."

Clark nodded, his eyes urging Tia to continue her story.

"I thought they made me more like her. She was so beautiful. I remember so many things about her. Her smile. Her laugh. How she always smelled like spring. When she spread her wings, I thought she looked like an angel."

"Where is she now?"

Tia's face clouded over. "My father hated her wings. He said they made her ugly. That no other man could ever want a woman with wings. It got a lot worse when she learned to fly."

Clark's jaw dropped open. "Your mom could fly?"

Tia stood. "Let's walk back. I'll tell you on the way." She idly leaned over and plucked up a dandelion from the small dirt patch at her feet. "I was only five the last time I saw her. But I remember it as if it's some video I rented and watched over and over."

"What happened?" Clark asked, as they started back.

"My father wouldn't let her fly. He even threatened to clip her wings. But when he wasn't around, she flew anyway. We lived outside of town then, so she could do it without anyone seeing her, if she didn't go far. One day he came home early and caught her. That night, I was asleep when their arguing woke me up. He must have been going after her. Then I heard glass shatter, and fluttering outside my window."

"It was her?" Clark asked.

Tia nodded. "The last thing I saw were her beautiful, lush wings spread against the moon as she flew away. I never saw her again."

"I'm sorry." Clark swallowed over the lump in his throat. "You must miss her."

"Every day." Tia stopped, and twirled the dandelion. "Do you think this flower is ugly?"

"No."

"Neither do I. I think it's beautiful. But a lot of people would just consider it an ugly weed." She threaded it through a buttonhole on his shirt, and smiled up at Clark. "It looks nice."

They started walking again. "When the wings started to grow, why didn't your mom go see a doctor?" Clark asked.

"We didn't have insurance or money for doctors. The first time I ever went to the doctor was when I was starting kindergarten. Besides, her wings were like this dark family secret. You know, shameful. At least that's what my dad said."

Clark pictured Tia's wings, as verdant as the ones she had described on her mother. The green feathers were the same shade of green as the meteorite.

"Are you sure you aren't grossed out?"

Clark prayed to find exactly the right words. "They're a part of you," he finally said. "And they're beautiful."

Tia's eyes grew luminous with unshed tears. "That's the nicest thing anyone ever said to me. Maybe if my dad had ever said something like that to my mom, she'd still be here."

"I'm sorry he didn't."

"Me, too. I think my dad's so strict with me because I look like my mom. He's afraid that if I grew wings, I'd fly away and leave him, too." Tia bit her own lower lip, deep in thought. "A person has to love you a lot to worry like that, don't you think, Clark?"

"I don't know," Clark said cautiously. "I mean, it's kind of like caging a bird who wants to be free. That's not really love, is it?"

"I never thought about it that way." She sighed. "Even if I wanted to fly away, where would I go?"

"I don't know."

They walked in silence for a while. Tia cast a sideways glance at Clark. "My father isn't a bad man. But if he found out about my wings . . ." She shuddered. "He'd lock me away, or worse. Anything to make sure I don't fly."

"I wouldn't let him hurt you," Clark insisted.

"You couldn't stop him. Not without telling about my secret. And I'd rather die than have everyone know I'm a freak of nature."

"I told you, Tia. I'll keep your secret."

She stopped and took Clark's arm. "I need you to swear. On the life of someone you love." She thought a moment. "On your mother's life."

"I can't do that," Clark said.

"I knew it." Tia's face clouded over. "I never should have trusted you."

"No. You can trust me."

She pulled away. "No, I can't trust anyone —"

"Tia." He grabbed both of her arms and held

them tight. "You don't have to be afraid. I'll do it. I'll swear."

She waited, her arms tense in his hands.

How can I not do it? Clark thought. *I owe her more than she'll ever know.*

He opened his mouth. "I swear on my mother's life, I will never tell anyone your secret."

"Thank you." She hugged him, and when she pulled away, tears shone in her eyes again. "I know I have no right to ask what I'm about to ask."

"What is it?"

"Well, I believe everything happens for a reason," Tia said. "After all these years, I'm growing wings, just like my mother. And you're the only person in the whole world who knows my secret. So I have to ask you . . ."

"It's okay. Go ahead."

She nodded. "Then here goes. Clark, will you help me learn to fly?"

CHAPTER 7

"How's work?" Martha asked Clark as he foraged in the back of the refrigerator for some pizza. The pie had come in as the last phone order of the night, but no one showed to pick it up. The Kents were eating a lot of free pizza these days.

"Fine." He flipped open the box and snapped a slice of veggie special. Meanwhile, his mom was removing all the spices from her cupboard and setting them on the counter. "What are you doing, Mom?"

"Reorganizing. There are four partially full containers of oregano. Now, would you care to elaborate on 'fine'?"

Clark got a plate for his cold pizza and sat down. "Let's just say that after working at this job, I see the value of an education so I never have to do anything this boring again."

Martha laughed. "From a mom point of view, that's good to hear. But you can bet you'll see your share of boring jobs when you're in college."

Clark took a thoughtful bite. "I'm working when I go to college?"

"Probably. I did. So did your dad," Martha said, as she uncovered two more containers on the top shelf. "Great. These never even got labeled. We can play Guess That Spice."

She unscrewed the top off of one and held it under Clark's nose.

"Marjoram."

"I'm impressed. Thanks."

"Mom?"

"Yes, Clark?"

"I don't even know what marjoram is," Clark confessed, with a boyish grin.

Martha laughed, shaking her head. "Ah yes, the famous Kent wit. Okay, we'll call it 'mystery spice.'" She wrote something on a piece of white tape and stuck it on the container. "Did you have fun with Tia yesterday?"

"It wasn't a date."

"I never said it was. I just asked if you had fun."

Well, it's like this, Mom. Tia's got wings and I've promised to teach her to fly. Me. The guy who's petrified of heights. The guy who's supposed to go skydiving with Pete and Lana and be happy about it.

"It was okay. Have you ever known anyone who tried skydiving, Mom?"

"A friend of mine in college. She ended up in the air force."

"Not exactly my first career choice," Clark said. He took an apple from the fruit bowl on the table and idly polished it.

"Maybe skydiving isn't the best idea for a kid with a thing about heights," Martha said.

"It'll be fine," he insisted. He couldn't admit to his mom that he was such a wuss.

Pete's not afraid. Neither is Lana. My fear is completely irrational. How can I be completely petrified about something so—

"Hey, Kents," Lex called. He was standing outside the screen door to the kitchen. "Can some-one help me? My hands are full."

Clark got up and loped over to let in Lex. "Lex. I didn't know you were coming over."

"I come bearing gifts." Lex held up a flat of sprouting plants as he stepped inside. "Baby toma-toes." He also had a brown burlap bag looped over his arm.

"That's nice of you, Lex," Martha said, "but we've already got tons of tomatoes in the ground."

Lex slid the flat onto the counter. "We've been doing some experiments at the factory. These plants came from seeds that originated in Greece. And *this,*" he said, indicating the bag he was car-rying, "is a new organic fertilizer that we're de-veloping. It's pricey, but we need to field-test it. I immediately thought of you."

Martha ran her hands under the faucet and dried them on a dishtowel. "I'm happy to help, Lex. If that fertilizer really is organic."

"It's a new formulation, specifically compatible with local soil. Completely natural. No artificial anything," Lex assured her. "Since I know you'll be wanting to use it, I left a dozen burlap bags of the stuff out by your barn."

"Attack of the Killer Tomatoes," Clark joshed. "Argh! They're eating the livestock."

"Your humor is slipping, Clark," Martha said, with a good-natured wink. "On that note, I leave to plant these seedlings. I just put some others in last weekend, so we'll see how they do head-to-head."

"Want help, Mom?" Clark asked.

Martha shook her head. "This won't take a minute. Why don't you offer Lex some iced tea? I'll be right back."

Clark opened the door for her, then turned back to his friend. "Want a slice?"

"Cold?" Lex made a face.

"It's an acquired taste. Free pizza is the only fringe benefit I get."

Lex leaned against the kitchen counter. "You know, if you wanted a job, Clark, you should have come to me. How much are they paying you at the pizzeria?"

"Not much," Clark admitted. "There's tips, though. That helps."

"If you want a decent job, there's always work to be done around the mansion," Lex said. "Or I could get you a position at the plant. Whatever Ellem is paying you, I'll pay double."

"Why?"

Lex laughed. "What are friends for?"

"Not to hire each other," Clark said. "That would make us employer and employee, instead of friends."

"Don't you think we could be both?"

"Sounds dicey. Thanks anyway."

Lex pointed at Clark. "That integrity of yours is an admirable quality. Who knows? You and I might run LuthorCorp together, someday. Stranger things have happened."

Not many, Clark thought.

"May I?" Lex asked. His hand hovered over the fruit bowl.

"Of course."

Lex plucked a pear. "So, you'll be glad to hear that we raised twenty thousand dollars at the carnival." He took a bite.

Clark whistled. "Impressive. That much, on homemade booths and raffle tickets?"

"I might have sweetened the pot somewhat," Lex admitted, chomping into the pear again. "But it's for a worthy cause. Speaking of raffle tickets, we're coming up on your skydiving debut, aren't we?"

"How did you know about that?"

"As I've pointed out on numerous occasions, there isn't much happening in Smallville that I don't know about. I was at the Talon, and Lana mentioned that you were in on it."

"What did she say, exactly?"

"That she can't wait to jump out of an airplane with you."

Great. I'm sure she'll be doing aerial back flips when I'm sobbing like a baby.

Lex grinned. "I think you'll enjoy it. I do."

"Wait. You've been skydiving?"

"Sure. More than once."

Maybe the more I hear about it, the less nervous I'll get.

"Tell me about it," Clark said eagerly.

"Well, when you first allow yourself to step out of the plane, it is amazing, especially the first time. It's like being . . . born. You're thousands of feet in the air, and you trust that you're not going to go hurtling to the earth. But the few seconds before your chute opens is an utterly adrenaline-pumping experience."

Clark felt the blood drain from his face. This wasn't helping.

"Clark? Are you okay?"

Clark hit his forehead with the palm of his hand. "What is wrong with me? Why am I so flipped out about this?"

"Clark?" Lex waited for an explanation.

"Okay, I have a confession to make." Clark's voice was low, not that there was anyone around to hear him. "I have this thing. About heights."

"This 'thing'?"

"Fear, you could say," Clark amended. "Of heights. Frankly, the truth is . . . I'm terrified. Petrified. I could barf just *thinking* about it."

"That bad, huh?"

"Worse," Clark moaned.

Lex threw his pear core into the trash can. "I could help."

"Doubtful."

"Clark, Clark, Clark," Lex chided him. "Am I not the guy who taught you how to tackle the role of *Cyrano* when you were certain you couldn't act?"

"True," Clark admitted.

"Well, then." Lex spread his hands expansively. "What are friends for?"

ꕥ ꕥ ꕥ ꕥ

How did I end up here?

"Great way to travel, isn't it, my boy?" Lionel Luthor yelled to Clark, over the loud *whup-whup* of the helicopter blades.

Clark nodded. He was afraid if he actually tried to speak, he'd beg like a little kid to climb down out of the chopper and back on the ground.

"Okay, Clark," Lionel Luthor shouted, "fasten your seat belt, put on your headset, and get ready for a birds-eye view of your hometown!"

Clark shot Lex a panicky look.

"I'd do as my father says," Lex said. "It doesn't get you very far to disobey him. It will be okay. Really."

Clark smiled grimly as he buckled himself into the four-passenger helicopter, thinking back on how quickly events had unfolded. It just so happened that Lex's father had come by company chopper to the LuthorCorp plant to do one of his periodic inspections. So, it had been an easy matter for Lex to ask his father to take him and Clark up on a quick reconnaissance flight. Lex hadn't said a word to his father about Clark's being nervous about flying, though.

The good thing about a helicopter, Lex had told Clark as they drove together to the plant, is that it could rise very, very gradually, even stopping to hover if Clark felt uncomfortable. It would be a way of baby-stepping into his fear. Lex had even suggested that if Clark truly felt panicked, he should just signal to him. Then, he'd tell his father that he, Lex, was feeling queasy.

"He expects it from me," Lex had confided, "even though I haven't been airsick since sixth grade. Funny how we all grow up, yet our parents seem to see us the way we used to be."

The engine that drove the rotors quickened,

pulling Clark from his musings. He darted a look at Lex, who was smiling confidently.

"This is a real pleasure," Lionel told Clark, his voice cracking over the headset. "Taking the son of Jonathan Kent up in the LuthorCorp helicopter. There really is hope for the world."

Clark forced a smile. He knew there was no love lost between his dad — who was one of the Smallvillians most suspicious of Lionel Luthor — and Lex's dad.

"Take it up slowly, Dad," Lex suggested. "Show Clark what this baby can do."

Lionel pulled back on the control lever with one hand and pushed the throttle forward with the other. The helicopter lurched into the air.

"Watch this gauge, Clark." Lionel pointed to the altimeter as the chopper rose. "It shows us how high we are off the ground. We go as high as five thousand feet."

Clark gulped hard. "Five thousand? That's certainly a lot of . . . feet, sir."

"You betcha!" Lionel agreed.

Clark's gaze shifted from the landscape to the

altimeter and back again, as the chopper gained altitude. Fifty feet. A hundred. The helicopter hovered, parallel with the roof of the LuthorCorp plant.

Okay, we're not up very high, Clark told himself. *It's not so bad. If I just remember to breathe deeply, that is.*

"You want to fly it, Clark?" Lionel asked.

"Um, no, sir," Clark answered. "You're the pilot."

"Good judgment. It's *not* as easy as riding a bicycle," Lionel told him. He took the helicopter up another fifty feet. Then another fifty. Then another fifty.

So far, so good, Clark thought. He risked another cautious look out the window. *I'm doing . . . okay. Really.*

He turned back to Lex, and gave his friend a cautious thumbs-up. Doing it gradually was working. Yes, he felt nervous, but the nerves were starting to give way to a kind of . . . almost . . . exhilaration. He was airborne. He was perfectly safe. Nothing was going to happen. He looked at Lionel, who was intent at the controls.

"Mr. Luthor?"

"Yes, Clark?"

"Could we fly over my family's farm? I'd love to see it from the air."

Lionel smiled at Clark. "If my son's friend wants to see his family farm from the air, then that will be our next stop!"

"No need to lay it on too thick, Dad," Lex said. "Your less-than-sterling-reputation has preceded you."

"I'm going to ignore that, Lex," Lionel said firmly. "It's unworthy of either of us."

Clark watched Lionel apply some gentle pressure on the tail rotor pedals on the floor of the chopper. It made the helicopter bank slightly and then zoom off to the southwest.

Ninety seconds later, they were hovering a thousand feet above the Kent farm.

Clark peered downward. There was the farmhouse, the barn, and the fields that spread out checkerboard-style on all sides. He could see Lana's house and the stables behind it. To the east was downtown Smallville, such as it was.

He smiled. He was such a part of this community. It filled him with warmth. What was it his father had once said . . . ?

"Everyone wants to belong, Clark. Everyone needs to be a part of something."

"Clark, look. I think your mother's waving at us!" Lex said, peering out the window. "Check out your driveway."

Now, Clark could see his mom, standing outside the front door to the farmhouse. She waved up at the LuthorCorp helicopter. Lionel piloted the chopper in a small circle to acknowledge her greeting.

"This is great," Clark said. "Thanks."

Lionel smiled. "You're welcome. So, Clark, would you like to come back to Metropolis with Lex and me for dinner? We'll have you home by nine o'clock, I promise."

"Can't, sir. Homework," Clark told him. "Thanks, anyway."

"Lex, did you hear what Clark said?" Lionel asked. "A boy in high school who thinks about his homework. Nothing like you at that age."

"You think, Dad?" Lex asked. Clark could hear barely disguised venom in his voice.

But if Lionel picked up his son's hostility, he didn't let on. "Let's circle around town, then put down," he told Clark. "So, you ready to invest in one of these?"

Clark smiled. "I think I'll try to save up for a used car, first."

"How are you doing, Clark?" Lex asked.

"Fine!" Clark was happy to realize that he meant it. The fear he'd felt was gone. Lex had been right — ascending gradually in the helicopter had done the trick.

Lionel turned the helicopter in a sweeping turn over Smallville's Main Street, past the high school, and back toward the LuthorCorp factory. That was when Clark realized something.

If I could have seen out of the spaceship, this is exactly what I would have witnessed when I plunged to Earth, just before my parents found me. Just before the meteorites pummeled this town, and killed Lana's parents, and —

"You sure you're okay, Clark?" Lex's hand was on Clark's shoulder. "You suddenly started looking a little green."

"I'm okay."

Lionel was in Smallville that day. What if he'd *found me instead of my parents? He'd be my father right now.*

Clark sat in silence as they descended toward the LuthorCorp helipad. Suddenly, a series of thunks shook the helicopter cabin, and the chopper jerked noticeably to the right.

"Dad?" Lex asked.

"Don't panic, Lex," Lionel said. But Clark's heart pounded and his stomach did a barrel roll as he saw how intensely Lionel worked the throttle and the controls, trying to get the helicopter back on an even keel. They were losing altitude in big chunks. In a matter of seconds, they had plummeted to two hundred feet.

And then, the engine quit.

"We can fly without the engine," Lionel declared. "It's called autorotation. But hang on. We're going to make a hard landing."

Clark looked down. Below wasn't the concrete helipad. Instead, they were above a field that ended with a steep embankment.

"Mayday, mayday, mayday!" Lionel declared into his radio as the helicopter descended.

Fear overtook Clark. He gasped as the altimeter swung back toward zero. One hundred fifty feet. One hundred. Falling fast.

I can't think about myself now, Clark realized. *What can I do to make sure everyone survives?*

Just like that, his fear was replaced by a sense of purpose and calm. He braced himself, preparing for the crash as the helicopter smacked into the field.

CRUNCH! The impact of machine against earth tossed Lex and Lionel against the wall of the chopper cabin and blew off the door on Clark's side. Then, Clark felt the chopper start to tip in his direction.

In a millisecond, Clark understood their predicament. They'd landed on the edge of the embankment. The helicopter was off-balance, in danger of tumbling end over end into a ravine. Moving so fast that the world seemed to stop around him, Clark flung himself out the busted door of the cabin, hoping that Lionel and Lex would think the forced landing was responsible.

Immediately he started to roll, but he jammed his hands into the ground to brake himself and then raced up to the teetering chopper. There, he dove under the dangling, ruptured strut and pushed with all his super-human strength.

The chopper lurched as Clark shoved it to stable ground. Then, with the machine safe, he tumbled back down the embankment into the ravine — exactly where he would have landed if he'd been thrown from the helicopter.

What to do now? Only one thing, he decided.

He closed his eyes, feigning unconsciousness, and waited for Lex and Lionel to come and "rescue" him.

Chapter 8

Clark closed the door to his bedroom — he didn't want either of his parents walking in and asking questions — and sat down at the computer. After the helicopter accident three days ago, they weren't too keen on Clark's continued plan to skydive. So he certainly didn't want them walking in on his how-to-fly research.

He was due to meet Tia in an hour at Raven Rock, not far from the dam just outside of town, for her first flying lesson. It suddenly occurred to him that he'd agreed to help her learn to do something he knew absolutely nothing about. Fortunately for him, he read really fast and retained pretty much everything he read.

Using an Internet search engine, Clark input the keywords "how birds fly." A slew of Web sites came up. He picked one, surfed in, and read the simple explanation:

> A gliding bird flies the same way as an airplane. The special airfoil shape of the wings, coupled with the bird's aerodynamic body, forces the air pressure above the wings to be lower than the pressure underneath. The difference in pressure creates lift, a physical force that acts perpendicular to the wing surface.
>
> Throughout history, humans have attempted to fly like birds, making wings out of all kinds of material. But the problem has not been the wings; it has been the musculature of humans, because we cannot create the relative strength of a bird.

I hope Tia's wings are stronger than her arms, Clark thought. He'd already been having second thoughts about this. Now that he was reading up on it, he was having third and fourth thoughts.

Like, for example, how the heck do birds take off in the first place? How do they keep from falling and breaking their bird necks?

He input new key words: "how birds take off,"

and started reading at the first Web site that was listed. It was actually really interesting. . . .

"Since when are you so interested in birds?" Chloe asked, startling Clark. He turned to find her peering over his shoulder, reading his computer screen.

"I didn't hear you come in." Clark clicked his screen to go dark. "Don't you believe in knocking?"

"I did; I guess you were too into bird-world to hear me. Writing a paper on toucans or something?" Chloe plopped down at the edge of Clark's bed.

"Just a little research."

"Weird coinkydink," Chloe remarked.

"What are you talking about?"

"This." She held up a green feather.

"You bought a parrot?" Clark guessed.

"Wrong-amundo. Whitney gave it to me." She twirled it between her fingers. "I suppose it would be more accurate to say that I *asked* him to give it to me. It's from the crime scene."

Clark frowned. "You mean when he was robbed?"

"As you know, Whitney never saw who attacked

him. All he found were a few green feathers. He told me he tried to give them to Smallville's finest when he reported the crime, but they were utterly uninterested. I, however, was *mucho* interested."

Clark took the feather from Chloe. It was the same color as the ones on Tia's wings. But Clark knew that Tia didn't have anything to do with the string of robberies. For one thing, her father barely let her out of the house. Still, the feathers looked so much like hers that it made him nervous. "What brilliant conclusion did you come to, Nancy Drew?"

"Very funny. I called the curator at the county bird sanctuary and asked if I could interview him. I'll show him a feather and see what he thinks. I'm on my way out there, now."

"What do you expect to find out?"

"A: What kind of bird has feathers like these, since I checked every field guide in the library and came up with zip. B: I dunno."

"You think a *bird* robbed Whitney?" Clark tried to sound as dubious as possible.

"Hel-lo, this is Smallville," Chloe reminded him. "*Anything* is possible."

"Hey, I've got it!" Clark exclaimed with mock enthusiasm. "It was Big Bird. Maybe Bert and Ernie were with him."

"And to think I was about to invite you to come along," Chloe said. She held out her hand for the feather, but Clark merely waved it like a metronome.

"Is this the only feather you have?" He asked.

"I have two. Why?"

"Mind if I keep this?"

Chloe folded her arms. "Why would you want it if my sleuthing is — ahem — for the birds?"

Clark winced. "Bad pun."

"Thank you. So, the feather?"

"Maybe it'll help me come up with some theory about what happened," Clark invented. "Think of it as inspiration."

"Come with me, we can get inspired together," Chloe suggested. "It's a really nice drive."

"Sorry. Got plans."

Chloe smiled smugly. "I know it doesn't involve a helicopter ride."

"You heard about the accident?"

"It's not every day a helicopter crashes in Smallville. I heard you got thrown all the way down a hill or something."

Clark shrugged. "The ground was soft."

"Yeah, but still. Did it put you off about skydiving?"

"No, I'm cool," Clark said, going for casual.

Chloe sucked her cheeks in. "So, you're not just doing this for L-A-N-A?"

"Why does everyone seem to forget that she's with W-H-I-T-N-E-Y?"

She dead-eyed him. "Why do you think, Clark?"

"Lana and I are just friends, Chloe."

"Gawd, I'm sick of hearing that," Chloe groaned. She sprang off his bed and headed for the door. "If you don't hear from me later, the monster green vulture at the sanctuary has gobbled the curator and is holding me hostage." She stopped at the door and turned back to him. "We still on for the picnic tomorrow, or are you busy with *plans* then, too?"

It took a moment for Clark to recall that Chloe had organized a picnic and disc golf match for the next afternoon, and he'd promised he'd be there.

But he'd also promised Tia that tomorrow would be her second flying lesson.

"I'll be there," Clark assured Chloe. "Oh, by the way, I'm bringing someone."

"I already invited Lana and she already said yes."

"Not Lana. Tia."

"Tia? As in, Tia-from-work Tia?" Chloe asked, surprised.

"Yeah."

Chloe waited for Clark to elaborate, but he didn't. "Is that yeah as in: you're-bringing-her-as-a-friend, or yeah as in: you're-bringing-her-as-a-date?" she queried.

"As in: a friend, not that it matters," Clark answered, as lightly as he could.

Chloe groaned. "Sometimes you make me insane, Clark Kent. Fine. Bring her. See you tomorrow." She slammed the door on her way out.

ᘐ ᘐ ᘐ ᘐ

Raven Rock was way off the beaten path, far from traffic and prying eyes. Clark figured learning to fly could be like learning to ski — first you

Maybe you psyched yourself into failing or
ıething."

Maybe," Tia mused. "I don't know why
ı're so nice to me, Clark."

If people knew you — other kids, I mean —
y'd be nice to you, too."

My father —"

'Right. I know all about your father."

'He thinks I'm at the library right now," Tia
ıfessed.

'Maybe I could talk to him and explain —"

'No!" Tia yelped. "Oh, no. That would be the
ırst thing."

"But you're going to have to stand up to him
entually," Clark reasoned. "The way he treats
u is just wrong."

"He's not a terrible person, Clark. And he's
art. Like he taught himself about the stock
ırket. He and my brother have been trading on
computer. Late nights; markets in Hong Kong
l London. That's how we could afford to move
ur new house."

ate nights? Markets in Hong Kong?

omething about that struck Clark.

had to tackle the aerial version of a bunny slope. Not that he'd ever been on skis.

They'd picked out a small bluff overlooking a field of wildflowers. Even if Tia fell, it was only about a three-foot drop. Clark knew he could catch Tia even if she fell from three hundred feet, but there was always that little matter of doing it without exposing his superpowers.

"Are you sure about this?" Clark asked her.

"Arboreal ancestors of a flying lineage," Tia stated.

"Does that have an English translation?"

"The ancestors of birds learned to fly by leaping from trees and spreading their wings," Tia translated. "My mom launched from the tree outside my window. If I can master this bluff, then I can move up to a tree."

"Okay. We know that an object moves farther and faster the harder it's pushed," Clark ticked off on his fingers, "and we know that if an object is pushed in one direction, there's always an equal resistance in the opposite direction."

"Thank you, Sir Isaac Newton," Tia said. "I don't think I'm ready for you to push me."

"I'm just reviewing the aerodynamic facts. You need enough acceleration to achieve lift."

Tia puffed some air from between her lips. "Well, Clark, I guess that's what we're here to find out." She took off her baggy shirt. Under it, she wore an athletic bra top that exposed her wings. She spread them wide.

Clark sucked in his breath. They unfurled almost to the length of her arms, the green feathers moving slightly in the breeze. As she turned around, he could see a complex maze of green veins leading to a fibrous muscled center.

Tia looked at Clark, uncertain of his reaction.

"They're beautiful," he told her.

She smiled luminously. "Thanks."

"Okay. You'll need to flap really hard and use that force to propel you forward. Then, just glide."

Tia put her hands on her stomach. "Suddenly, I feel kind of sick." She laughed nervously.

"I'll be below. If you fall, I'll catch you."

Tia nodded. "I'll take a running start." Clark descended to the bottom of the hill. Tia backed up twenty feet. Then she ran toward the edge of

the bluff, flapping her wings as hard as sh
and launched herself into the air.

Flapping wildly, hovering . . .

Clark peered upward, arms outstretche
fling this way and that to stay underne

"Harder!" Clark yelled. "You can do it!

With a cry of frustration, Tia fell, la
Clark's arms.

"Thanks," she told him breathlessly.

"You weren't very high, it was easy." H
put her on the ground.

Tia retracted her wings. "Failure num
huh?"

"But you didn't fall right away," Clar
out. "I bet you'll do better and better e
we practice."

"I doubt it. What was I thinking? I

"You've only tried once. I really thi
do it, Tia."

She looked puzzled. "It's weird.
you yelled up to me that I could do
in my head said, 'No, you can't.'
I fell."

"Umm . . . didn't you tell me that the only reason he let you work for Ellem is because your family needed the money?"

"That's why he let me get the job in the first place," Tia explained. "They just started this trading thing. My dad says they're really making a lot of money at it."

Maybe the money for the new house didn't come from stock trading, Clark thought. *Maybe it came from robbing people at night. From above. It's awfully far-fetched, but . . .*

"Tia, does your dad have wings?"

"Not a chance. If he had wings, he and my mom could have flown together, and she wouldn't have left us."

"Yeah," Clark softly agreed. "But what if he grew them recently?"

"I don't think so."

"Have you seen his back in, say, the last few weeks?"

Tia frowned. "No. We're a pretty private family."

"Keep your eyes open," Clark advised. "But be careful."

"Okay, I will. But no matter what you think of

my father, Clark, he's the parent who stayed. That means a lot." Tia checked her watch. "One more try. Then, I've got to go."

"This could be it," Clark encouraged her.

She wrinkled her nose. "Why do I feel like telling you that I'm going to fail every time you try to encourage me?"

"I don't know," Clark admitted. "But I'm not giving up on you. Tomorrow, we'll come back for lesson two."

"Are you sure?"

"I promised, didn't I? Afterward, my friends are having a picnic in the park. Come with us."

"Really?" she asked shyly.

Clark nodded firmly. "Your dad can't keep you from having friends, Tia."

"I'll ask about the picnic, not about the flying," Tia decided.

"Fair enough," Clark agreed.

"Fair enough." And she climbed up the bluff to try again.

Chapter 9

The next day, Tia made sure her door was locked, then threw off her nightgown and stepped into her jeans. She was meeting Clark in an hour at the library, then they'd go off on another flying lesson. After that, he was taking her to a picnic with his friends. She was so excited, imagining it would be like what she saw on TV, where teenage girls had friends — even boyfriends — and worried about silly things like their clothes or their hair . . . instead of worrying that someone would discover their wings.

She double-checked the door again, then stood in front of the mirror on her dresser and spread her wings in all their green glory. How could Clark find them beautiful? She tried to see them through his eyes. Impossible. She'd heard for years that her mother's wings had been ugly and shameful. It was hard to get her father's messages out of her head.

Tia sighed as she gazed at her reflection. She could still hide her wings by retracting them, but they seemed to be growing daily. The feathers were getting thicker and darker, the sinews of the wings themselves stronger. The bigger they got, the more shameful she found them.

Yet Clark Kent found them beautiful.

In Tia's mind, the word "beauty" described a girl like Lana Lang. She'd watch Lana at school, sometimes, and wonder what it would be like to be that lovely, that in control. Perfect, really.

Fat chance she'd ever find out.

She was startled by a knock on her door. "Who is it?"

"Shake a leg if you want a ride to the library," her father said coldly.

"I'll be right out," she called back.

Her heart was still hammering. The idea of her father finding out about her wings terrified her.

He'd never hit her, though he had come close many times. But if he found out the truth, Tia was pretty sure he'd hurt her.

As for him having wings, well, Clark would be happy to know that he didn't. Even though theirs was a very private family — she couldn't remember the last time she'd even seen her brother or father in a bathing suit — she'd held a mirror in front of his cracked bedroom door as he undressed for bed. She got enough of a glimpse of his back — pale pink, smooth as a sheet of plastic — and knew that Clark's suspicions were ill-founded.

Now, she wrapped a large ace bandage around her chest and back to cover her wings, then put on a baggy T-shirt and an even baggier sweater. On a whim, instead of braiding her hair, she left it loose, flowing over her shoulders. Then she smiled at herself in the mirror, trying to imagine how Clark and his friends would like that smile.

"Hey sis? Get your butt out here!" She heard Kyle's foot connect hard against her door.

"Just a sec!" She grabbed her purse and joined

her brother. "You don't need to batter down my door."

Kyle shrugged. "What were you doing in there? It's not like you need to make yourself pretty."

Something about the way Kyle had said the words made Tia feel hopeful. Maybe it was because she was wearing her hair loose instead of in its usual braid. "You mean, because I already am pretty?"

"Yeah. Pretty ugly," Kyle snorted. "Now get your skinny butt out to the car before Dad gets any madder than he is already." He loped for the door.

Someday, Tia thought, *I will fly away, and my life will be beautiful.*

Someday soon. If I ever do figure out how to fly.

ꕥꕥꕥꕥ

"Flap harder, Tia!" Clark called to her through his cupped hands. Tia was hovering five feet above the field like some kind of beautiful, gigantic hummingbird. But no matter what she did, she couldn't seem to move forward.

"I can't!"

As soon as Tia said "can't," her wings stopped moving and she plunged toward the ground. Clark caught her easily and put her down. It was the tenth time he'd done so that morning.

"Tia, as soon as you say you can't do it —"

"I know, Clark. I'm sorry."

"Don't be so hard on yourself."

"What's the use?" Tia put her head in her hands, green feathers spread like some kind of preternatural angel. "I'm ugly and stupid and I can't do anything."

"Maybe the only reason you can't do it is because you don't believe in yourself," Clark said quietly. "You said so yourself, remember?"

She didn't reply. Clark was reasonably sure that he was right. He'd measured her wingspan and read as much as he could about aerodynamics. From everything he could figure out, it was theoretically possible for her to fly.

"Think, Tia," Clark went on. "You're already

able to keep yourself in the air like a helicopter." The irony of the comparison wasn't lost on Clark, not that he planned to go up in a helicopter again any time soon. "So you're not that far from flying."

She lifted her head, eyes full of doubt. "You think?"

He nodded.

"When I'm home, I lock my door and work on building up the muscles in my back and wings. I know they're stronger, but . . ." She shrugged helplessly.

"You're going to do it," Clark insisted. "How about if after the picnic this afternoon, we come back and try again?"

She blinked hard. "You'd do that for me?"

"Sure."

She gave him a quick hug. "You're the best friend I ever had, Clark. I don't know how I'll ever repay you."

Clark smiled. "Just be a great friend to someone else. How's that?"

ꕥ ꕥ ꕥ ꕥ

"Who ate the last drumstick?" Pete demanded as he rummaged in the giant cooler.

"If memory serves correctly, you did," Chloe pointed out. "Not that anyone's counting."

"I'll have you know I'm packing on the pounds in anticipation of my forthcoming growth spurt," Pete explained. He pointed from Clark to Whitney. "Watch it, guys. I'll be looking down at you very soon."

"I think you look fine just the way you are," Tia said shyly.

"Now see, this girl has taste," Pete announced. He jumped up from the blanket. "Who's up for a little Frisbee?"

"I'm in," Whitney said, getting to his feet. He stretched and threw an imaginary touchdown pass.

Lana hugged him, her arms lingering around his neck. "I'm glad you came out with us today."

He gazed at her. "Yeah?"

"Yeah. You've been working long hours while you're home on leave from the Army."

"And missing you," Whitney murmured.

Clark tried to look everywhere except at the dismal sight of Lana with her arms around Whitney's neck, gazing soulfully into his eyes.

"Yo, Clark! Frisbee?" Pete asked, spinning the orange disc on his index finger.

"Yeah, sure. Want to play, Tia?" Clark asked.

She shook her head. "I don't think so. But you go."

"You sure?"

"She can hang with us," Chloe assured Clark.

Lana arched a brow. "Wait, the guys are playing, and the girls are staying?"

"It's so *Brady Bunch* I could puke," Chloe teased. "Go on, you guys. We don't want to make you look bad."

"Yeah, right," Pete scoffed.

Chloe scrambled to her feet and motioned for the Frisbee. Pete tossed it to her. "Clark, go long!" Chloe shouted. As Clark jogged away from her, Chloe spun the disc to him.

"Nice one," Clark called, catching it and sailing it back to her.

"One lucky throw," Pete told Chloe.

Chloe rolled her eyes. "To think that I'm rising to your weenie bait." She called to Clark again. "Go way out, okay?"

Clark complied and called to Chloe through cupped hands. "Go for it!"

"You can't —" Pete began.

But Chloe had already snapped her wrist and let the disc fly. She'd tilted it a little sideways, so it arched neatly to the left and then spun gracefully downward to Clark.

Nice, Clark thought, jockeying slightly for position so that he'd catch the disc when it fell. *Accurate, too.*

He snagged the Frisbee, wondering how far and accurately he could throw it if he really let loose. His whole body itched to do it. He could imagine everyone's shock at his talent. Lana would be so impressed. She'd put her arms around his neck, and smile up at him, and —

"Clark! You playing or dreaming?" Pete shouted.

"Here it comes," Clark called, and sailed the Frisbee toward Pete.

"You guys up for disc golf?" Whitney asked

when Clark rejoined them. He cut his eyes at Chloe. "Don't tell me, you're great at that, too."

"I've proved myself enough for one day, thanks," Chloe said, plopping back down on the blanket. She flashed a radiant smile at Tia as the guys jogged off toward the disc golf course at the other end of the park. "So, Tia. How are you and Clark getting along?"

Tia popped open a soft drink. "What do you mean?"

Chloe began collecting picnic debris and stuffing it into a plastic garbage bag. "Oh, you know. Do you like hanging out with him?"

"That's Chloe-speak for 'are you dating Clark?'" Lana clarified.

"Lana!" Chloe objected. "If I wanted to know that, I'd just come right out and ask. So, Tia: Are you dating Clark?"

Tia laughed so hard that she snorted the soda she was drinking through her nose. "Oh. God, I'm sorry!"

Between peals of laughter, Chloe and Lana tried to assure her it was all right.

Tia mopped up the soft drink. "Well, now you've seen me at my worst."

"Believe me, my worst is infinitely worse than your worst," Chloe assured her. She rolled onto her stomach, chin propped in her hands. "I have this charming habit of being mortifyingly blunt. For instance, Clark said your mom split when you were a little kid. Is that true?"

"You're prying, Chloe," Lana admonished, then looked back at Tia. "She has a tendency to approach life like an investigative journalist. Try to ignore her."

"I don't mind." Tia fiddled with the metal tab on her soda can. "It's true. I don't know where my mom is. It's not much of a story. I mean, I miss her, but . . ." Tia's voice trailed off. Then she shrugged. "It's not like I can do anything about it."

"I know the feeling," Lana said softly.

"That's right," Tia realized. She knew Lana's history. "It would be easier if my mom was dead, in a certain way."

Lana shuddered. "Now, that's a gruesome conclusion."

"What I mean is, you know your mom would be with you if she could be," Tia explained. "When I was little, I thought my mom was my guardian angel. But then she took off, left me behind, and never came back again."

Chloe and Lana were silent. They had no idea what to say.

"At least you still have your dad," Chloe finally said. "Lana doesn't have that."

"Oh please, let's not throw me a pity party," Lana groaned.

Tia smiled. "If it makes you feel any better, my father is so strict I had to lie to him about what I was doing this afternoon. He wouldn't even let me be with you guys, if he knew."

"Get out!" Chloe couldn't believe it. "Why?"

Tia shrugged. "It's just the way he is."

"But a picnic? In the park? On a Sunday afternoon?" Lana wondered. "You're sixteen, not six."

"Tell *him* that," Tia sighed. "He thinks I'll turn out like my mom. According to him, she was wild." She shook her hair back and raised her face to the afternoon sun.

"Wow, you've got gorgeous hair," Chloe said. She scooted behind Tia and got on her knees, lifting the hair off Tia's neck to put it up in a ponytail.

"Don't!" Tia sprang away from Chloe as if she'd just received an electric shock.

"What?" Chloe asked, alarmed. "What'd I do?"

Tia backed away. "I'm sorry. I just — I don't like people to . . . touch my hair."

Chloe held her palms up. "Hey, sorry. It was a middle school knee-jerk reflex, leftover from my pajama party days. I didn't mean anything."

"No, I'm sorry. It's me, not you," Tia insisted, blushing.

"Have you ever cut it?" Lana asked, hoping to smooth things over.

Tia didn't move. "When I was little. Now my father won't let me."

"What is up with him?" Chloe exclaimed.

"I told you, he's —"

"Yeah, yeah, strict. We got it." Chloe said impatiently. "But it's *your* hair. You should be able to dye it green, if you want to."

Tia laughed. "Well, I don't want to."

"But you get my point," Chloe insisted.

"Believe me, it would be lost on my father."

Chloe felt indignant on Tia's behalf. "Stand up to him."

"It's not that easy."

Lana nudged Chloe's arm. "Quit pressing her."

"I'm not pressing. I'm merely offering ideas for home improvement," Chloe explained. "And she never answered the question about her and Clark, by the by." She turned to Tia. "So?"

Tia shrugged. "We're just . . . hanging out."

"'Hanging out' can mean anything from everything to nothing," Chloe remarked. "Maybe you could be more specific?"

"We're friends," Tia said.

"Okay, that phrase should be banned from the English language," Chloe groused.

"Give it a rest, Chloe," Lana suggested. She shielded her eyes from the sun and watched Whitney chuck a Frisbee to Clark. They were warming up before they started their disc golf match. "It's so great to see Whitney out having fun. Ever since his dad got sick, his life totally changed." She turned to Chloe. "Get this. The police called him down to the station house and interviewed him again about the robbery. He's *still* a suspect."

"Oh, that reminds me." Chloe reached for her purse and rummaged through it until she brought out a green feather. "Ta-da!"

"What does that mean?" Lana asked.

"It means I took this feather to the bird sanctuary. And the curator told me it's not from any bird he's ever seen. Not in Kansas, not anywhere. Pretty weird, huh?"

Tia felt her heart thudding in her chest. The feather Chloe was holding looked just like her own.

But she hadn't been anywhere near Whitney that night.

"Um . . . where . . . where did you get that?" Tia hoped her voice wasn't trembling too much.

"Whitney found it at the crime scene, the night he was robbed," Chloe explained. "So, anyway, the curator took a few tufts from the feather and he's having them tested." She stuffed the feather back into her purse and raised her eyebrows at Lana. "And so, the mystery deepens."

"Maybe it's from someone's hat," Tia said nervously. "You don't know that it's from the robbery. It could have just been on the street. Right?"

"Right," Chloe agreed. "But somehow I doubt it."

"Tia!" A voice boomed.

All three girls looked up as Mr. Haines marched toward them, eyes blazing.

Tia jumped up. "Dad! What are you doing here?"

He stood before her and stabbed the air with an accusatory finger. "I dropped you off at the library. You were supposed to stay there."

"How did you —?"

"Find you, you little sneak? The librarian told me she saw you go off with the Kent boy; she said she overheard something about a picnic in the park. What do you have to say for yourself?"

Tia went blotchy with embarrassment. "We can talk about it at home."

"You lying little —"

Chloe and Lana were on their feet. "Mr. Haines,

there's no reason for you to talk to her that way," Lana interrupted. "We were just having a picnic."

Mr. Haines narrowed his eyes at Lana. "You stay out of it. I know your kind."

"What?" Lana's jaw dropped open in disbelief.

Chloe was indignant. "You can't talk to her like that!"

"I didn't ask your opinion," Mr. Haines spat, then he grabbed his daughter's arm. "You have a lot of explaining to do, young lady."

"Dad, please —" Tia began softly.

"Mr. Haines, stop." Clark's voice was soft, but commanding.

The man turned to see Clark standing behind him, with Whitney and Pete on his flanks. The three young men stood their ground with quiet strength.

"Kent. I should have known," Mr. Haines growled. He turned to his daughter. "You're sniffing after him like a dog in heat. Just like your mother."

Clark came closer. "Don't talk to her that way." His voice was steely.

Mr. Haines got in Clark's face. "You talking to me, punk?"

"My name is Clark, *sir.* And yes, I'm talking to you."

"Don't interfere, Kent," Mr. Haines warned, then yanked so hard on Tia's arm that she winced in pain.

Anger bubbled up in Clark. He reached for the older man's bicep in one quick motion. "You're hurting her, Mr. Haines. Let her go." Clark squeezed the bicep. Very hard.

"Ouch!" Mr. Haines howled in pain and jerked away from Clark. "Who the hell do you think you are? You don't know who you're messing with, punk. I can make you sorry you were ever born."

"I don't think so, Mr. Haines. I don't respond very well to threats."

"That is not a threat, punk. It's a promise." He pivoted toward his daughter. "Say good-bye to the Kent kid for the last time, Tia. Because as of right now, he's out of your life."

Chapter 10

Smallville Pizza was depressingly empty. Clark refilled the sugar canisters. Then he swept the floor, wondering exactly what was going on in the back room between Ellem and Mr. Haines.

It was the day after the picnic; Tia hadn't been at school that day. Clark and Lana had called her house at lunch, but there was no answer. Then, when Clark came into work to start his shift, Mr. Haines had showed up instead of Tia.

Suddenly, the door to the back office slammed open. Mr. Haines strode out, Ellem at his heels. "You're a fine one to talk about Kent's character," Ellem fumed. "He happens to be an upstanding young man. It's your character in question here. You treat that lovely daughter of yours like dirt."

"What I do with my family is none of your business. You're just an ignorant foreigner. We shouldn't even let your kind in."

That comment made Clark see red. But even though Ellem came up to Mr. Haines's chin, Clark knew that his boss was more than capable of handling himself. In fact, now Ellem was getting right in Mr. Haines's face.

"You listen to me, you big bully." Ellem's quiet tone belied the fury in his eyes. "You can force your daughter to quit. You can spread all the lies you want to about me and my employees, since no one will believe a word out of your lying mouth. But I'm warning you. You lay one finger on Tia and you'll be answering to me and Big Max. Have I made myself abundantly clear?"

He'll be answering to me too, Clark thought. *And he definitely doesn't want that.*

"Get the hell away from me, you little slug," Mr. Haines sneered. Then he turned on his heel and stomped out of the restaurant.

Ellem unconsciously flexed his fist. "It would give me great satisfaction to knock the stuffing out of that man," he said, as the door closed.

"I know the feeling," Clark agreed. "Did he tell you he made Tia quit because of me?"

"Something like that."

"I feel kind of guilty. We were on a picnic yesterday with some friends when Tia was supposed to be at the library."

"For the love of God, the girl is sixteen years old. Since when is a Sunday picnic a mortal sin?" Ellem asked rhetorically. "Get the topping vats from the walk-in, will you, Clark?"

Clark brought out the pepperoni and cheese vats; Ellem was still fuming as he ran long pepperoni sausages through a meat slicer.

"The world can be a harsh place, Clark," Ellem sighed. He jammed another pepperoni against the whirring metal blade and watched it disappear into a pile of thin slices. "A very harsh place, indeed."

ঔঔঔঔ

"Hey, son. How was work?" Jonathan asked when he came downstairs later that evening and found his son standing in front of the refrigerator, drinking milk directly from the carton.

Clark took a half dozen of his mom's freshly baked oatmeal cookies from the cookie sheet on which they were cooling and handed three to his dad. Then they sat at the kitchen table, and Clark filled in his father on Tia and Mr. Haines.

"Haines sounds like he's got a few loose screws," Jonathan said, chewing thoughtfully on a cookie. "Do you think he's physically abusing his daughter?"

"I don't know, Dad. He's rough, but Tia said he doesn't hit her."

"She might be lying," Jonathan mused. "Believe it or not, sometimes kids do that to protect an abusive parent. Especially when it's the only parent they've got."

That made sense to Clark. Tia had even said something about her dad being the only parent she had. Now he felt even worse about the situation. "Dad, I have to do something."

"You can't go around accusing people of child abuse when you don't have any proof, Clark. Be careful with this."

"So what am I supposed to do, nothing? Tia's a really nice girl, Dad."

Jonathan went to the refrigerator for the milk carton, then reached into the cupboard for a couple of glasses. "In case your mom walks in," he said, referring to the glasses, since they both preferred drinking milk right out of the carton. It drove Martha crazy. "Where's Tia's mom in all this?"

"She . . . left."

Jonathan poured the milk and handed his son a glass. "You mean she abandoned her family?"

Clark nodded. "A long time ago."

"Sounds like the whole family is messed up."

"You don't know the half of it, Dad."

Jonathan folded his arms. "I'm listening. Tell me."

I wish I could, Clark thought. *I'm so used to confiding in you and mom about this kind of stuff. If I could tell you, you'd understand why I feel responsible for Tia's horrible life. And why I swore on mom's life that I'd keep Tia's secret.*

"It's confidential," Clark finally muttered.

His father's eyebrows rose. "Clark, are you and Tia involved?"

"You mean romantically? No. She's my friend.

I care about her. I can't just stand by and do nothing, Dad."

"Hey, you two," Martha called from upstairs. "It's after eleven. Let's hit the hay. Or I'll throw some of Lex Luthor's magic fertilizer on you. It burned up the tomato plants he gave me."

"Spoken like a farmer's wife," Jonathan called back. "We'll be right up." He turned back to his son. "Let me talk this over with your mom. Step one, let's see if Tia's in school tomorrow. If she's still missing, and you can't reach her by phone, we'll go over to her house together, okay?"

Clark agreed. He put their glasses in the sink, then trudged upstairs behind his father. He wasn't feeling very hopeful. Unless he could tell his parents the truth about Tia, he knew it would be difficult for them to help him. But he was not going to betray Tia, no matter what.

CHAPTER 11

The next evening, Clark was taking a break at the pizzeria when Chloe blew in, very excited.

"So listen to this, Clark," she said, sliding into the booth across from where he was nursing a cup of coffee. "The bird sanctuary curator finished his tests on the green feather I gave him. He said the DNA in it was all messed up — like something had caused some kind of mutation."

"From the meteorites, probably," Clark said.

So if the meteorite dust is responsible for Tia's mutation, and Tia didn't rob Whitney, then someone else has the same mutation.

"Clark? You still with me here?" Chloe called.

Clark blinked. "Yeah. Sorry. Just thinking."

"Me, too. I'm with you on the meteorite theory.

But how do we connect a mutated feather with a robbery?"

"Got me," Clark said.

"I'm thinking . . . a person got dosed with meteorite dust twelve years ago and grew feathers," Chloe mused. "And this guy can fly. Or girl. It could be a girl."

"Call the tabloids on that one," Clark scoffed, hoping to throw Chloe off track from the female angle. 'I'm a Bird-Woman Prom Queen' can go right next to 'Boy Crashes to Earth in Artichoke-Shaped Spaceship.'"

"You, of all people, Clark, should remain scoff-free when it comes to the weirdness that is our cozy little burg." She reached for his coffee and took a sip. "So, did you tell your dad how Tia wasn't at school again?"

"I'll tell him when I see him. He wasn't there when I got home." Clark idly tried to balance the saltshaker on a single grain of salt. "I'm thinking maybe I should check it out myself, make sure she's okay. Ellem must have her address."

"It's the house with the blue shutters at the

end of Jayhawk Road, in the new LuthorCorp subdivision. I looked it up this afternoon. Don't bother to thank me, that's what friends are for," she added with a sweet smile. "I'll even go out there with you."

"That's okay, I can't go until after work, it'll be late, you know how it is," Clark said all in a rush.

Chloe shot him a killer look. "If you don't want me to go with you, just say so, Clark."

"No, it's not that."

"Because I thought you and Tia were just buds. But if it's more than that, tell me. It's not such a big deal, you know."

"It's . . . complicated."

Chloe folded her arms. "Thank you for the clarification, Mr. Cryptic."

Clark looked at her directly, his piercing eyes locked on hers. "I'm sorry, Chloe. Really. If I could explain, I would. But I just can't."

"Yeah. Okay. It used to be a lot simpler to be friends. Before high school and dating and who's zooming who, you know?"

Clark pushed the saltshaker back toward the

pepper and sugar containers. “Maybe that's just how life is, Chloe. You get older. It gets more complicated.”

Chloe was silent for a moment. “Yeah,” she finally agreed. “But don't you sometimes wish it didn't have to be?”

It's always been that way for me, Chloe, is what Clark thought.

But he said, “Yeah, Chloe. You can't imagine how much I wish that.”

ఙ ఙ ఙ ఙ

“Clark, me boy, we need to talk.” Ellem wiped his hands on his apron, then took it off and slung it over his shoulder.

Not now. Any other time but now.

Clark was in the cramped back room, about to punch out at the end of his shift. As much as he liked Ellem, he desperately wanted to leave. He'd tried to call Tia a half dozen times during the evening, but there was no answer, and no machine picked up. He was really starting to worry. He planned to go to her house as soon as he got out of the restaurant, whether his father could come with him or not.

"What's up, Ellem?"

"Well, Clark, there's a problem."

What'd I do? Clark wondered, doing a quick mental inventory of his shift. *There were hardly any customers. I filled the salt- and pepper shakers, sorted silverware, restocked the straws, and got so bored I wanted to scream. Maybe my distraction was showing. I hope not.*

"Tell me what it is. I'll fix it," Clark said firmly.

Ellem scratched his head self-consciously. "The fact of the matter is, I've got to let you go. I'm laying you off."

"You're *what?*"

Ellem held up his hand. "Now before you get your gym shorts in a wad, hear me out. Big Max applied for a wine and beer license and it finally came through. We're putting in a bar, ferns in the window, a real Italian menu with a real chef. You know, class the place up."

"But everyone loves this place the way it is," Clark protested.

"How many customers did you serve tonight,

Clark? You could count 'em on one hand, and the lovebirds that came in after the movies nursed a slice for an hour. Fact is, every day and night of the week except Saturday we're hemorrhaging business to the Talon. That place has Luthor money behind it — we can't compete. Big Max and I want to go for a more adult image. So we're changing the name to Ellem on Main, and hiring help over the age of twenty-one."

He put a hand on Clark's shoulder. "No hard feelings? I think the world of you, Clark."

Now that Clark was over his initial shock, he actually felt like jumping for joy, although he knew that in his case such a leap could send him through the ceiling. He'd already earned enough money for skydiving, and working at the pizzeria had gotten terribly monotonous.

But quitting would go against the Kent follow-through-on-your-commitments credo. In other words, my parents would have had a fit.

Clark cleared his throat and put on an appropriately solemn face. "No hard feelings, Ellem." He put out his hand. Ellem shook it.

"You're a great kid, Clark. Sorry I didn't give you more notice. But I hated breaking it to you, so I put it off."

"I understand."

Ellem snapped his fingers. "I know. I'm giving you a leave-taking bonus."

"You don't have to do that," Clark protested.

"Hell's bells, Clark, it's the least I can do, letting you go without notice and all. Wait right here."

Ellem hustled to the back office and returned with an envelope, which he handed to Clark. "There you go, me boy. I'll write you a great letter of recommendation if you need one. You've always got friends in me and Big Max, forever and a day."

Clark thanked him and stuck the envelope in the back pocket of his jeans.

"Ready to go? I'm set to lock up. Just leave your apron here; we'll be remodeling tomorrow, starting at seven A.M." Ellem tapped a big envelope that he was also carrying. "Just going to make the night deposit, then get me some shut-eye."

Together, Clark and his boss closed down the

place; Clark took one final nostalgic look at it before Ellem turned out the lights.

Ellem on Main. Nothing stays the same. Not even in Smallville.

Once they were outside, Ellem locked the deadbolt. "Well, Clark, here's where we part. When the renovations are done, bring the parents in for a —"

WHAM! Something from above slammed into Clark with the force of a city bus. Despite his superstrength, the impact knocked him sideways. He crashed through the front of the pizzeria, shattering it into a lethal confetti of flying glass.

"Help!"

Clark lifted himself up to see Ellem outside on the ground, swinging his arms and legs wildly against two attackers. They were clad in black, with black stocking caps on their heads.

Clark sprang to his feet and leaped through the mangled glass shards. He dove at one of the assailants, smashing him into the middle of the street. Then he turned to the other criminal, grabbed him by the arms, and hurled him away from the storefront. The man's body arced through the air; Clark had aimed for him to land in a heap near his cohort.

Only he didn't land at all.

Instead, at the top of the arc, powerful green wings spread out through a hole in the man's shirt. He flapped them madly, hovering above Main Street like some kind of demonic mythological creature.

Clark gasped when he recognized the malevolent face of Mr. Haines through the stocking cap.

"Get up, son!" he yelled down to his partner, who still lay dazed in the street.

That must be Tia's brother, Kyle, Clark realized. *But Tia told me that her father didn't have wings! Is she in on everything with them? Am I being played for the biggest sap in the world?*

Ellem leaned against the building, unconscious, blood running down his face from a serious gash near his hairline. His left leg was bleeding badly where a glass shard had ripped through his pants leg.

With a shake to clear his head, Kyle flapped his wings; he rose into the sky and joined his father.

I could easily jump and reach them, Clark realized. *But Ellem needs help. He's losing a lot of blood.*

He knelt beside Ellem and applied direct pressure to his leg wound, helpless as Mr. Haines and his son flew off into the night.

CHAPTER 12

"Tia? Tia!" Clark yelled, as he pounded on the front door at the Haines home. He was sure the police were only a few minutes behind him and he wanted to get to Tia before they did. He'd bandaged up Ellem, called the police, and then told them on their arrival that he'd seen the attackers — Mr. Haines and Kyle — but that they'd gotten away.

He left out the part about them flying. As for Ellem, he was too woozy from his loss of blood to give any statement at all.

"Tia!" Clark yelled, louder this time. "Are you in there?"

There was no answer. But there was so much that Clark had to figure out. He checked the door to see if it were unlocked. It was.

Cautiously, he stepped inside. "Tia?" he called. "Tia! Are you here?"

Clark super-sped through the house, checking every room. No one was home. In Tia's room he saw a broken window, which didn't make any sense at all. Then, in the master bedroom, Clark skid-stopped at an odd sight: two light pink, plastic prostheses were on the floor. They approximated the size and shape of the human back.

I get it now. No wonder Tia thought that her father didn't have wings. He and Kyle must have had these plastic prostheses special ordered. They wear them to stop anyone from getting suspicious. Then they take them off to do their airborne crimes.

In the master bedroom was a locked door. Clark smacked it with his shoulder and knocked it down. An amazing sight greeted him: stacks of checks from the various businesses that had been robbed, including Fordman's Department Store, plus credit card slips and cash.

There's the proof, Clark thought, and decided it would be wisest not to touch the evidence. *At least now Whitney's name will be cleared. I don't adore the guy, but I don't want him arrested for something he didn't do, either.*

From far away, he heard the wail of a siren. The police were on their way. Clark didn't want to be there when they showed up. They could take care of the evidence. Meanwhile, there was the question of Tia.

Where was she? Had her father and brother taken her away? And if so, what did they have in store for her? Clark knew he had to find her before it was too late.

ᏡᏡᏡᏡ

"Clark, we were so worried!" Martha cried, moments after Clark had zoomed home and into the kitchen. "The police called from the pizza place. They said you and Ellem had been attacked. But when we got down there, you were gone."

Clark filled them in, including the fact that Mr. Haines and his son had emerald wings and could fly, which was how they had committed all the nighttime robberies.

His mother paled. "Emerald green, you said? The same color as —"

Clark nodded. "It has to be some kind of bizarre mutation from the meteorites." He made a tight fist of frustration — there was so much pressure and guilt bottled up inside of him. "When will it ever end?"

"Clark, it isn't your fault," Martha said.

"No, actually it is," Clark lamented. "Whatever brought me here brought the meteorites, too. So many people have been hurt, Mom."

"You were a baby," Jonathan reminded him. "A baby is innocent, Clark."

Clark shook his head. "I just don't know anymore."

"Did you feel sick when you were near Mr. Haines, like you feel sick around the meteorites, son?" his father asked.

"No. I think Mr. Haines and his son are mutated, not poisoned. It's Tia I'm worried about."

Jonathan looked directly at Clark. "What, does she have wings, too?"

Clark shook his head, wishing yet again that

he could tell his parents about Tia's wings. But he couldn't. No matter what.

"I can't tell you that. I made a promise."

"Clark," his father began. "How can we help you if you don't tell us the truth?"

"I just can't," Clark said. "Not right now."

"That is simply not an acceptable answer," Jonathan responded. "When does 'not right now' end?"

Clark swallowed hard, feeling incredibly conflicted. He hated that he couldn't share everything with his parents.

"How about . . . tomorrow night? If I can't find her."

Martha looked at Jonathan. They came to some unspoken agreement.

"I think I figured out the answer to the question I asked you," Jonathan said. "Go find your . . . look, Clark. Is there something more going on here between you and Tia?"

"Nothing, Dad." Clark saw the look that passed between his parents. He knew he didn't sound very convincing.

"If I only knew where to look, where she might have gone . . ." Clark didn't finish the statement. As far as he knew, Tia didn't have any friends. Except him.

"It's been a hard night, Clark," his father said, "and it's late. There's nothing any of us — including you — can do until the morning. Get some sleep."

Clark trudged up to his room, got ready for bed, and crawled between the sheets. He felt like a failure.

I let Tia down. What good is it to want to help someone when you can't figure where she'd go to if she was in trouble or —

The idea hit Clark so suddenly that he bolted upright in bed. He *did* know where she was. Stealthily, he pulled on his clothes, pushed into his sneakers, and zoomed downstairs.

CHAPTER 13

S*ometimes when I really feel alone, I go there and think about how vast the universe is . . . and somehow it makes me feel less alone. Looking at the stars like that.*

As he rushed to the loft in his barn, the words he'd said to Tia came flooding back to him. He was sure that he'd find here there.

"Tia? I know you're here. It's okay."

Clark stood in the center of his loft, calling softly. He could have used his X-ray vision to find Tia, but he figured it was better to let her come to him.

A light flipped on in the corner.

There was Tia, wearing an old sweatshirt and jeans, sitting in an ancient red velvet chair Clark had rescued during the renovation of the Talon. Her knees were drawn up to her chest like a little kid. There was a small stack of envelopes at her feet.

"How'd you know I was here?" Tia asked.

"Lucky guess." He went over to her and knelt. "Are you okay?"

She nodded yes, but her lower lip quivered, and tears began to spill down her cheeks.

Wondering how much Tia knew about what had happened that night, Clark got the roll of paper towels he kept in the loft for the rare occasions when he cleaned up, and handed her a sheet. "Sorry, it's not exactly a handkerchief."

"That's okay." Tia dabbed at her eyes and blew her nose. "This was the worst night of my life. I had a terrible fight with my father. About you."

"Me?" Clark pointed at himself.

Tia nodded. "It's not your fault. He thinks I'm hiding some big love affair from him. He just kept screaming at me, worse than he ever has before. He threatened me with scissors."

Clark gasped. "Tia, did he hurt you?"

"Only my heart." She turned her head, and Clark could see that her father had chopped off

Tia's beautiful hair at the nape of her neck. "Then he locked me in my room."

"How did you get away?"

Tia blew her nose again. "I heard him and Kyle leave really late. Then I kicked out my window and climbed down. It was dark, I don't think anyone saw me. I hope. Then I came here. I didn't have anyplace else to go."

"It's okay." Clark put his arms around her, and she sobbed into his chest while he comforted her.

Finally, she lifted her head, and dried her eyes on her sleeve. "I'm sorry, Clark. There's no reason my problems should be your problems."

If you only knew, Clark thought.

"You're my friend, Tia. I care about you."

"My father looked crazy, Clark. I mean it. I've never seen him like that before. Once he finds out I'm gone, I think he'll do anything to get me back." She grabbed Clark's arm. "You have to be careful. I'm sure he's going to come here looking for me."

"Actually, I don't think that's very likely."

That was when Clark told her the story of the

evening — the attack at the pizza parlor on himself and Ellem, how he went to the Haines house and found the plastic prostheses and all the evidence from the other robberies.

"Oh my God," Tia breathed. "My father and brother —?"

"Have wings, too," Clark said.

"I swear to you, I had no idea."

Clark nodded. "I believe you."

Tia just shook her head. "And I believed my dad when he said they made money in the stock market. How could I be such an idiot?"

"Don't say that. It's natural to want to think your parent is telling you the truth. Don't blame yourself."

Tia jumped up. "I've got to get out of here. This means I've really put you in danger. I know my father and Kyle will find me here." Her eyes darted around, as if trying to figure out where she could go.

"Calm down. Every cop in Kansas is going to be on the lookout for them. I don't think they'd risk coming here. They're on the run. Or on the flight, so to speak. You're safe."

"Do you think the police will think I'm a criminal, too?"

"No. I'm sure they're looking for you, though. You weren't in school, you're not at home . . ."

"They'll think my father did something horrible to me," Tia concluded.

Clark nodded. "Look, Tia, there's something we have to talk about. I know I gave you my word that I wouldn't tell anyone about your secret, and I won't go back on that. But we have to figure out what to do."

She gave him a half-serious smile. "Couldn't I just live in your loft?"

"My parents are already suspicious. They're going to find out sooner or later that you're out here. I've been thinking about your mom. If only we could contact her."

Tia smiled. She reached for the envelopes scattered on the floor. "Well, maybe there's good news. Yesterday, I went down to the basement. My dad has an old trunk down there. This is what I found." She held out the envelopes. "Letters from my mom to me."

"Tia! That's so great."

"Yeah." She smiled sadly. "She's been writing to me for years, and my dad has been intercepting the mail. I guess he kept them because he's still in love with her. Or is it because he's so filled with hate? I'm so mixed up."

"It doesn't matter. What it means is, we can contact your mom. Why don't you look more excited? Isn't this exactly what you wanted?"

Tia shook her head. "It's not that simple." She unfolded the most recent letter and began to read.

Dear Tia,

I know, even as I write to you, that you can never write back to me. To give you my address would put both of us in danger. Your father so hates my wings that if he found me, I know he'd try to kill me. Leaving you broke my heart, Tia, but I did it to save my life. Selfishly, I wish you had grown wings, too, so that we could have flown away together. But without them, I felt the best thing for me to do was to leave you behind and let you have a normal life. Know that I will always love and miss you, and wish with all my heart that you could find your way to me. In my dreams, we're flying together, safe and free. I love you very, very much.

MOM

Tia gave Clark a luminous smile. "She loves me. I always thought she didn't, but she's loved me all along." Tia dropped her baggy flannel shirt from her shoulders and freed her wings from the sides of her sleeveless T-shirt, unfurling them in all their glory. "I wish she could see this."

"Maybe she can, someday."

"How? I can't fly, Clark."

"You're your mother's daughter," Clark said firmly. "I believe you can." He held out his hand. "May I see the rest of those letters?"

Tia handed them to him. He scanned the postmarks. There were clusters of different ones. Some from North Carolina, from a few years ago. A bunch from Minnesota. The latest batch all seemed to be from Colorado. There were a couple from Granby, from someplace called Kettering, even from Boulder.

An idea formed in Clark's mind as he handed her back the letters.

"You can stay here overnight. Tomorrow, we can try to find your mom."

"How?"

"I've got an idea. We can discuss it in the morning. But Tia, if we can't find her, then I have to tell my parents." Clark's voice was steady. "If you're here, they're involved, too."

"I never should have made you swear on your mother's life in the first place," Tia admitted. "I was scared."

"So, do we have a deal?"

"Yes." Tia leaned over and kissed Clark on the cheek. "Lana is a really lucky girl."

"Why do you say that?"

"Because she has your heart."

For once I'm not going to say 'Lana is with Whitney,' Clark thought. *For once, I'm just going to tell the truth.*

The words "You're right, Lana Lang does have my heart" were on the tip of Clark's tongue. He opened his mouth to speak. And out of nowhere, as if he'd somehow conjured her up, he heard Lana's voice.

"Clark?"

Lana stood at the top of the stairs, gaping at Tia. Instantly, Tia retracted her wings and pulled her shirt back up on her shoulders, eyes round with fear.

"I couldn't sleep, so I went for a walk," Lana began. "I saw your light on up here . . ." She faltered.

"You can't tell anyone what you just saw," Tia begged.

"What *did* I see?" Lana asked. "Am I dreaming, or do you have wings?"

"Yes," Tia finally answered. "I do. Are you going to tell?"

Lana sighed, and shared a glance with Clark. Clark knew what she was thinking: Yet another one of the weird things that happens in Smallville. Maybe weirder than most. But still . . .

"Of course not," Lana replied firmly. "I only wish I had known sooner. It must be tough to keep such a big secret. Guys are nice, but it's hard if you don't have a girlfriend you can confide in."

"I wouldn't know," Tia admitted. "I've never had one."

Lana smiled at Tia. "Well," she said, "now you do."

"Tia, tell Lana what happened tonight," Clark said. "I'm going back to the house to get you a sleeping bag. Are you hungry?"

Tia nodded.

"And a sandwich. Be right back, okay?"

"Okay," Tia agreed, yawning. "Thanks, Clark. I mean it."

ꕥ ꕥ ꕥ ꕥ

By the time Clark came back to the loft a couple of minutes later, Lana was waiting outside.

"Everything all right?" he asked her.

"Wings, Clark? Lana asked. "Tia has grown wings?"

Clark shook his head. "I know, it's almost unbelievable."

"You live here in Smallville long enough, nothing is unbelievable. Or at least that's what I'm starting to believe. Anyway, she fell asleep," Lana said simply. She shivered. "I covered her in my jacket."

Instantly, Clark removed his own sweater and handed it to her.

"Won't you be cold, Clark?"

"Nah," he smiled. "I'm impervious."

Lana put the sweater on — the arms hung past her hands. "I feel as if I intruded on something private just now," she began. "I just . . . when I saw the light in your loft, I was sure you were alone. I'm sorry."

"I'm not."

"I know the loft is special to you, Clark. If Tia is up there . . . well, I guess that means she's special to you, too."

Is Lana trying to find out how I feel about Tia?

"I found her hiding in my loft," Clark explained. "I didn't take her there."

He hesitated a moment, unsure of how to say what he wanted to say; unsure of whether or not he should say it at all.

Some people say you can love more than one person

at a time — romantically, I mean. Maybe some people really can do that. Maybe even you, Lana.

But I can't do that. Not me.

No. He could never say that aloud.

"I don't love her, Lana."

Lana's dark eyes shone in the moonlight. "Do you believe in destiny, Clark?"

"I don't know. Why?"

"Because sometimes I just get the strongest feeling that you're destined for something . . . I don't know . . . bigger than I can even imagine," Lana said. "And I think that it could be even bigger than the feelings you have for . . . well, anyone."

"No, I don't believe that," Clark said fervently.

But deep down, his biggest fear was that Lana could be right.

ଓଓଓଓ

"I can't believe you told Lana and you didn't tell me," Chloe griped as she turned onto the dirt road that lead to the headquarters of the county bird sanctuary. "I would have been on this sooner."

It was after school the next day. After Tia agreed that Clark could enlist Chloe in the effort to find her mother, Clark had invited Chloe to the loft. Chloe thought Tia's wings were about the coolest thing she'd ever seen, and she immediately agreed to help. And when Clark had suggested trying to track down any recent reports of giant bird sightings in Colorado, Chloe had suggested that they go to the bird sanctuary and talk to the curator.

"Clark didn't tell me," Lana explained from the seat next to Chloe. "I walked in on them last night. In the loft."

"Oh." Chloe blew a bubblegum bubble, then popped it. "So, you just wandered over to Clark's loft in the middle of the night?"

"I had insomnia."

"Cozy," Chloe remarked as the car bumped along the winding road. "Anyway, about the curator. His name is Dr. Scott Dievendorf. He looks like this kid I had a crush on in third grade back in Metropolis, only grown up."

"And he's a bird expert," Lana assumed.

"More than that," Chloe said. "He's obsessed.

He knows pretty much everything there is to know about anything — real or mechanical — that flies. Frankly, I think what he really wants is to be able to fly, himself."

She pulled into the parking lot of the sanctuary headquarters, which was no more than a modified warehouse. Once inside, Chloe gave their names to the girl behind the reception desk, who told them that Dr. Dievendorf was waiting for them in the central aviary.

The cavernous room, filled with flora and fauna, trilled with bird songs. Flashes of brightly colored plumage winged over their heads as birds flew from tree to tree.

"I can't believe I've never come out here before," Lana said. "It's amazing."

Chloe found the curator sitting on a stone bench, a parrot perched on one shoulder and a finch on the other. She introduced him to her friends.

"So, two visits in one week, young lady. What can I help you with?" the curator asked.

"We were wondering if you knew anything about sightings of any unusual birds in Colorado,"

Clark began, careful not to give away too much information.

"Unusual in what way?" Dr. Dievendorf asked as a canary landed and perched on his outstretched finger.

"Very large," Clark went on. "The size of a human. With feathers like the one Chloe brought to you. I realize it's a long shot, sir."

"Why are you asking?" the curator inquired.

"He's doing a research paper on urban legends," Chloe replied quickly. "The kind that end up in the tabloids. Bigfoot. Sasquatch. Like that."

The curator stood and the canary took wing from his finger. "Come with me." He led them down a corridor, the finch and parrot still on his shoulders, then opened the door to his cramped private office. The walls were covered with photos and charts.

"Leonardo da Vinci, 1485," the curator said, pointing at a drawing of giant batlike wings atop a small flying machine. "He called that an ornithopter." He moved down a few feet and tapped a framed drawing of a crude air glider. "George

Cayley. Two centuries ago, he worked on creating a human-powered glider."

"It's really interesting, sir," Chloe said politely. "But what does it have to do with a big green flying thing, now?"

"Forgive me," Dr. Dievendorf demurred. "Flight is my passion. All my life, I've dreamed of flying. And now you ask me about this half-bird, half-human winged creature in Colorado. It's amazing."

"You mean there really is one?" Chloe blurted out.

He picked up a copy of a tabloid that was on his desk and handed it to Clark. The headline: GREEN ANGEL-WOMAN SIGHTED!

Clark tore through the pages, until he saw a blurry photo of a female form aloft, massive wings outstretched.

"The photo was taken three months ago by a tourist at Rocky Mountain National Park, north of Granby, Colorado," Dr. Dievendorf explained. "He hiked so far into the back country that he got lost. Right at dawn, he saw this in the sky and snapped the photo. He said the creature had green feathers, but since the picture is black and white, you can't tell. No one believes his photo is real, by the way."

"Do you believe it's real?" Lana asked him.

He took the tabloid back and gazed at the photo. "If I didn't, I wouldn't give it to you to see. Isn't she beautiful?" He turned to Chloe. "The green feather you gave me to analyze was such a vivid hue; I remember thinking the color looked electric. *As if it glowed.*"

"Wow," Chloe said nervously. "Imagine that."

"Did you sight her in Smallville?" Dr. Dievendorf asked eagerly. "Is that how you got the feather? What's really going on here?"

"Like I told you, it's a school paper," Chloe insisted. "Wow, look at the time." She feigned a quick look at her watch. "So listen, we have to run. You've been really helpful, sir."

When they left the curator's office, he was still staring longingly at the Bird Woman's photo. Once they were outside, Lana asked, "What do you guys think?"

"I think," Clark said, "that we just found Tia's mother."

Chapter 14

"It's time," Clark told Tia.

She looked outside at the evening sky. That afternoon, Clark, Lana, and Chloe had brought Tia a map; they had highlighted the least populated route from Smallville, Kansas to Rocky Mountain National Park. Clark was sure that Mrs. Haines was somewhere in the park. They'd planned that at nightfall, Clark alone would help Tia take flight.

But now that the time had come, she was petrified. "I don't think I can do it, Clark."

"You can, Tia. Your mom is waiting for you. Remember, if the police ask me, I'm going to tell them the truth. That you told me you went to your mother, but I don't exactly know where your mom is."

"And when I get to Colorado," she said tentatively, "my mom and I will contact the police there."

"That's right," Clark affirmed.

She nodded, but didn't look convinced. "I still don't know if I can do this."

"I know it's scary," Clark reassured her. "I bet you didn't know that I hate heights, too."

"You do? You never told me that."

"Sometimes I think we get tested by whatever scares us the most. And if we pass that test, then we end up where we're really supposed to be."

She smiled weakly. "You're full of philosophy, Clark."

"Or just full of it." He handed Tia a black knit cap. Lana had purchased it at Fordman's along with the black pants and black sweater, which she modified to allow Tia's wings to spread freely. Wearing this ensemble, Tia would be less visible at night. "Come on, let's do it."

"What if I can't fly?" Tia asked. "I've never been able to before."

"Tonight's the night," Clark said. "I just feel it."

They headed downstairs and outside. Clark had set up a klieg light that had been in the garage since he threw that impromptu party the time his parents had gone to Metropolis. It lit up the area around the barn nicely — if Tia couldn't take off from the barn roof, Clark wanted to be certain he could see well enough to catch her.

Good thing my parents are at a farmers' cooperative meeting tonight. So I have a little time to figure out what to tell them, if worse comes to worst. Because if Tia's still here when they get back, it's truth time.

Tia stood at the foot of the ladder that led to the roof of the barn. "So, this is it," she said nervously. "Hug me for luck?"

Clark enveloped her in his strong arms. "Your father can't stop you anymore, Tia," he whispered into her hair. "You can fly. You can."

She nodded into his flannel shirt, then pulled away. "Thank you for being the best friend any girl ever had. I'll never forget you, Clark." She reached for the ladder.

WHAM! From out of the night, Clark was smashed to the ground in a flurry of wind and a pounding on his head.

Immediately, Clark knew.

Mr. Haines and Kyle. They've come back! And they're after Tia!

"Tia!" Clark shouted. But Kyle had already grabbed her as Clark found himself lifted into the air by Mr. Haines, who was flapping his powerful wings against the night sky.

As if anticipating that Clark could get away from him, Mr. Haines hissed, "Make a move and she dies." He flew higher and higher still, holding Clark in a viselike grip.

Twenty feet. Thirty. Forty. A hundred feet in the air! The wind felt frigid against Clark's skin. He looked down — below him was the roof of the barn. He felt dizzy and light-headed, all his fear of heights bubbling to the surface, but he refused to give in to it. He had to concentrate on Tia.

Clark closed his eyes, hoping that would help the vertigo. "Tia's your daughter," he reasoned, "I know you don't really want to hurt her."

"I'll do whatever I have to do," Mr. Haines growled. "She is not going to do to us what her mother did."

"Just leave! If you go, you'll never have to see

her again," Clark pleaded as Mr. Haines took him higher into the dark heavens.

"Shut up! I should have gotten rid of her a long time ago. Just like I'm getting rid of you. Have a nice death, punk."

Mr. Haines let go of Clark. He plummeted from the sky, helpless, terrified, and smashed headfirst through the wooden roof of the barn, and then into several bales of hay on the barn floor.

It was a fall that would have killed any mortal. But Clark merely pushed himself up from the hay bales, marveling that he was completely unhurt.

Until he heard Tia scream from outside.

He ran at superspeed. But it was too late. Holding Tia between them, Mr. Haines and Kyle were airborne with the sobbing girl.

"Clark, help me!" Tia cried.

There was nothing he could do. He stood there helplessly as her father and brother rose higher and higher. They were too high for him to reach them by jumping. Even if he scaled the barn and leapt at them from the shattered roof, he couldn't reach them.

I can't let Tia die. There has to be a way to save her.

That's when his eyes lit on the steel trash cans outside the barn.

The lids looked like giant Frisbees. Clark got an idea.

Let this work. Please. Let this work.

Clark snatched the covers off both cans. He held them by their rims, flipping them over his back, one in each hand, so that they looked almost like a butterfly's wings. He eyed Tia's dangling form, calculating how quickly her father and brother were flying and in what direction. He was firing at a moving target, and if his aim were off even a little, it could be disastrous for Tia. But it was a chance he had to take.

Clark slung the lids skyward, the compact saucers soaring upward at incredible speed. One lethal disc hit Mr. Haines's wings, the other one, Kyle's. They screamed with pain and reached instinctively for their smashed wings, losing their grip on Tia.

"Fly, Tia!" Clark shouted up to her. "Fly!"

She flapped her wings frantically, hanging in

mid-air, neither moving forward nor backward, as her father and brother tumbled to the earth.

Clark was waiting. He caught Mr. Haines first, then Kyle, and threw them against the barn. Then he grabbed a coil of rope that was by the side of the barn. Quickly, he bound the two men together, standing back to back. Now, Clark could turn his attention back to Tia, who was still hovering above, spinning in a circle, eerily reminiscent of Lionel Luthor's helicopter before its crash landing.

"Fly, Tia!" Clark shouted upward. "Fly, now!"

"I can't do it," Tia moaned. "I can't!"

"Yes, you can, Tia. Do what scares you!"

For a long moment, Tia hovered, somewhere between believing the lies she'd been told about herself and embracing the truth about boundless possibilities. And then, a miracle happened. Tia started to move forward.

"Go! Go!" Clark's heart soared with his friend's wings. He watched, transfixed, as Tia made a half-circle around the barn, then turned in the other direction and smoothly swooped down toward him, hovering just a few feet above the ground near her bound father and brother.

"Good-bye, Dad."

"Don't you dare —" her father began.

"You'll never have the chance to say that to me again." Tia interrupted, her voice strong. "I *do* dare. You were right all along. I'm just like my mother."

With that, Tia rose higher into the air; all her father could do was shake an impotent fist at her. He lost his balance; father and son toppled directly onto one of the open canvas sacks of supercharged LuthorCorp fertilizer that Lex had brought the week before. A big cloud of pulverized dust rose around them.

"Go, Tia," Clark urged as his friend swooped in graceful circles just over his head. "Fly as far as you can until daybreak, then lay low and fly again at night."

She plucked a single feather from her wing and let it flutter down to Clark. "Keep it with you. It's your good luck charm."

Clark smiled. "I will."

"I thought my mother was my guardian angel, Clark," she told him. "But I was wrong. You are." And with that, she ascended into the inky sky, spiraling higher and higher, until she became one with the night.

Wow. She did it.

"Help me," Mr. Haines moaned weakly.

Clark whirled. The two men were still where they'd fallen, atop the LuthorCorp fertilizer pile. But something weird was happening. Clark realized that their wings were shriveling before his eyes.

Something in the fertilizer is destroying their wings, Clark realized. *Didn't my mom say that the fertilizer burned out her tomato plants? It's burning out their wings, too!*

He pulled the men off the burlap sacks, watching in amazement as the wings continued to wither and blacken . . . and finally, turn to dust.

"I'm sick, Dad," Kyle said.

"Call an ambulance," Mr. Haines whispered hoarsely.

"I'll do that," Clark assured him. "Right after I call the police."

Clark super-sped inside the barn, found more rope and the portable telephone, and dashed back outside again.

"How'd you do that so fast?" Mr. Haines croaked.

"Magic." Then, just in case Mr. Haines and Kyle gained their strength, Clark bound them together further by their hands and feet.

"You stole my daughter away from me," Mr. Haines growled at Clark.

"You're wrong, Mr. Haines," Clark said as he punched in the number of the police station. "You tried to keep her in a cage. But Tia finally set herself free."

Epilogue

"I can't believe you're missing out," Lana said into her cell phone to Pete. She and Clark stood in the shade of one of the modified Quonset huts that serviced Smallville's tiny airstrip.

"If I ever tell you I'm going to eat potato salad at my cousin Cheryl's house, stop me," Pete said. "In fact, stop my whole family. We all got food poisoning and we've only got two bathrooms. It isn't pretty. Hey, put Clark on, okay?"

Lana handed Clark the phone.

"Hey, buddy," Clark said. "How are you feeling?"

"About five pounds lighter. So much for packing it on in anticipation of a growth spurt," Pete replied. "Listen, I wanted to wish you bon voyage. You still freaking about this?"

Clark cast a quick glance at Lana. "Semi," he replied.

"Just think — you, Lana, and the friendly skies, it's got to be good. Uh oh, my stomach is declaring war again. Gotta go. Hang tough, my man."

As Clark handed the phone back to Lana, Terry Waters, their lead skydiving instructor, strode over to them. "Five minutes. You guys ready?"

"Absolutely," Lana said. Clark managed a weak thumbs-up.

Terry nodded approvingly. "Good, 'cause we're all set for you. The team is out at the drop zone, the plane's ready, you're geared up and good to go. Smile, Clark. It's going to be an experience you'll never forget. I'll be back for you in five."

Lana peered at Clark. "You look kind of pale. I hope you're not getting sick on me, too."

"I'm fine," Clark assured her, although his stomach was doing flip-flops. He'd thought that the daylong skydiving training they'd gone through together would be more than sufficient to cure any lingering butterflies he had about jumping out of an airplane. But he was wrong.

It wasn't as if Terry, Janet, and the team hadn't

thoroughly trained them. He and Lana had watched a training video, then were shown all the gear they'd be using and how it worked. They'd had a session on the specially designed harness, and on how to steer a parachute after it opened. They'd even jumped out of a mock airplane and done endless drills of pulling their rip cords and checking their altimeters. Clark knew it all. Heck, he could teach it to somebody else.

Now if only that somebody else was the one jumping out of the actual airplane at 10,000 feet, instead of me.

Lana peered at the cobalt blue sky. She raised her arms as if they were wings. "Imagine being able to spread your wings and fly, like Tia. Wouldn't that be amazing?"

Clark made an appropriate grunt of agreement.

"I finally read *Jonathan Livingston Seagull,* you know," Lana said. "It was beyond corny. But in a sweet way. Whenever I think of it, I'll think of Tia. At least her dad and brother are in jail. She doesn't have to worry about them anymore. I keep hoping that we'll get a postcard or something, so we'll know she made it to her mom."

"Tia and her mom were supposed to go to the police when she got to Colorado. The sheriff here won't tell me anything, though. Because I'm not family," Clark said.

"You think she made it?" Lana asked.

"I think it was her destiny. Just like —"

Before Clark could finish his answer, Terry was heading back over to them. "Let's get ready to rumble!" he called.

Lana nudged Clark playfully. "There's nothing to worry about. Even if everything fails, you've got that automatic thingie on your chest that pops the reserve chute at a thousand feet."

Clark gulped hard. "Gee. That makes me feel so much better."

"We're jumping with two instructors," Lana reminded him. "One on either side of us. If your rip cord doesn't open the chute, they won't let go."

Their first jump would be the "Accelerated Free-fall Method." That meant they would leap off the plane with two instructors, who would flank them until their chutes opened. Then, the instructors would let go and free-fall before opening their own chutes; a radio headset would guide Clark and Lana to the drop zone.

Clark heard the airplane engines firing up on the other side of the Quonset hut. By the time Clark and Lana got there, the plane's single propeller was whirring loudly. Janet was in the pilot's seat in the cockpit. She gave them a cheerful wave.

Clark felt nauseated. Why couldn't he be the one who had food poisoning?

Terry reached down to help Clark and Lana into the plane, where the three other instructors waited with parachutes already on their backs.

Someone else was on board too, equally packed and ready to go.

Lex.

"What are you doing here?" Clark blurted out.

"Nice to see you, Clark," Lex said wryly. "You too, Lana. I believe I mentioned that I'm a certified skydiver. I haven't had a chance to jump recently. So I asked Janet and Terry if I might tag along. I hope you won't mind."

"Fine by me," Lana said. She went off with Terry to get her chute secured to her back. Lex edged closer to Clark as one of the other instructors helped Clark into his gear.

"I didn't show up here to rain on your parade with the fair Lana," Lex told Clark, his voice low. "I came for moral support."

"Believe me, I'm glad," Clark murmured. "I need all the moral support I can get."

"I hope the mishap in my father's helicopter didn't exacerbate the fear factor."

"Frankly," Clark said, "it didn't help."

"For what it's worth, I'm sorry. I'll make it up to you."

"It's not your fault. Sometimes stuff just happens."

"Not to me, Clark. I like to think I control my destiny." The edges of Lex's mouth rose in a quirky smile. "Funny, though. How often we have to do the thing we most fear to get to whatever that destiny might be. Ever feel that way?"

One of the instructors clapped Clark on his bicep before Clark could respond. "You're all set there."

"Thanks." Clark turned to Lex. "I can say with

great conviction and even greater certainty, Lex, that flying will *never* be my destiny."

Lex peered out the window. "Life can be full of amazing surprises. *Never* say never."

ꝏ ꝏ ꝏ ꝏ

"Eleven thousand feet!" Terry shouted back from the cockpit over the noisy engine. "Let's get ready to do it! Lex, you're first!"

Clark wished with every fiber of his unusual being that he were anyplace but where he was: in a plane, about to jump from it.

Terry opened the door and checked to see that they were approaching the drop zone.

"Good luck, Lex!" Lana shouted.

Even in his petrified state, Clark could see that Lana was practically glowing with excitement. God, she was just so beautiful. And fearless. People expected her to be a wimp because she was so petite and fragile-looking. But Clark knew that on the inside, Lana was a heavyweight.

It's one of the things I love about her. And loving her

is how I ended up in this stupid plane with this stupid parachute strapped to my back.

"Okay, perfect position!" Terry told Lex. "Ready to go for it?"

Lex nodded. But instead of heading for the door, he leaned close to Clark and spoke in his ear. "You can do it, Clark. I believe in you." Then he climbed out of the plane, onto the support strut under the right wing. As Clark and Lana had been warned in training, Janet shut down the engine. They were gliding now, eleven thousand feet above the green fields of Kansas.

"Go!" Terry shouted. And Lex was gone.

Clark and Lana watched as Lex free-fell. Seconds ticked by. Then, the chute popped open; Lex floated gently in the sky. By then, Janet had restarted the engines, and was circling back for another pass over the drop zone.

Lana turned to Clark. "I'm so glad you're here."

"I'm . . . glad I'm here, too," Clark replied.

"Lana!" Terry shouted. "You're up!"

Lana covered Clark's hand with her own. "You're the bravest person I've ever met, Clark.

When someone is in danger, you risk your life to save a life. If I were in danger now, you wouldn't think twice about jumping out of this plane."

She's right, Clark realized.

Terry opened the cabin door, and Lana waited as one of the other instructors clambered out onto the strut. Then, she followed, trailed by a second instructor. Together, the three of them braced themselves against the wind.

And then Lana and her two instructors leapt into nothingness. Clark watched, transfixed, as the three of them plunged earthward.

WHOOSH! Lana's chute popped open. As it did, Clark saw the two instructors drop away, into their own free falls.

"Clark!" Terry called. "You're up."

Janet steered the plane back over the drop zone. Terry led the way out onto the wing strut. Clark followed, willing himself not to look down. Behind Clark came Tammy Connors, the second instructor. For a brief moment, the three of them crouched out on the strut, battered by the wind.

Do what they taught you, Clark told himself. *Just do it. If Lana was in danger, you'd do it in a nanosecond.*

"I'm ready!" Clark shouted into the wind.

Both the instructors gave him a thumbs-up.

Funny how often we have to overcome our biggest fear to face our destiny.

An image of Tia standing on the grassy knoll near the dam came to Clark; how scared she had looked, how hopeless. Clark's believing in her had helped her to finally believe in herself. Which is what Lex and Lana had just done for him.

You can do it, he told himself.

"Go!" he shouted to the instructors, and he let go of the wing support.

He was flying.

Or, at least, it felt like flying. For the briefest moment, a wondrous power and joy stronger than anything he'd ever known coursed through Clark's body. In his mind, his parachute, the instructors, even the plane, disappeared. He was alone, soaring through time and space.

I belong here.

In the next instant, everything Terry had taught him and Lana came back to Clark — he knew to arch his back and spread his arms and legs, in order to stop his body from tumbling out of control during the free fall. He checked his altimeter so that he would know when to deploy his chute.

"Nine thousand feet!" he yelled to Terry. Then he turned to Tammy and gave her an okay signal. Just as he'd been taught to do, he demonstrated a couple of practice pulls at the rip cord for them, to show that he was in control. And then, at 5,500 feet, he signaled that he was ready.

WHAM. He yanked the rip cord at a mile high. *WHOOSH!* The chute opened like a giant blossoming flower, with Clark at the stem. His instructors dropped off. He was all alone. Silent. Gently falling toward Earth, utterly free.

A shadow darkened Clark's face. He looked up.

A beautiful green-winged bird-woman glided above him.

Tia!

And then, with sinewy wings of the most brilliant emerald, Tia's mother swooped down from the sky, making majestic circles around her daughter and Clark.

Clark waved. Tia came closer, and waved back.

Clark reached into the pocket of his jumpsuit. He pulled out the green feather that Tia had given him for luck. He held it aloft. She was close enough to see it. And she gave him the biggest thumbs-up ever when she did.

Clark thought the air had never smelled so fresh, nor had a sky ever looked quite so blue as it did in that moment, as he floated toward the earth. He watched Tia and her mother spiral upward, further and further still, until they disappeared into cerulean infinity, where anything was possible.

With the wind against his skin, surrounded by perfect silence, Clark thought: *I will remember this moment forever. This is what joy feels like.*

It feels like flying.

About the Authors

Cherie Bennett and Jeff Gottesfeld are a well-known writing couple, authors of several award-winning novels for young adults. Cherie is also one of the nation's leading playwrights for teens, a two-time winner of the Kennedy Center's "New Visions/New Voices" award. As part of the inaugural writing staff for *Smallville*, they wrote the first season episode, "Jitters." They answer all their email personally; learn more about them at their Web site, cheriebennett.com.

PRINTED IN U.S.A.
GAYLORD